I DO REMEMBER
THE FALL

I DO REMEMBER THE FALL

THE EXILE CLASSICS SERIES, NUMBER THIRTY

M.T. KELLY

INTRODUCTION BY STEPHEN WILLIAMS

DRAWINGS BY CATHERINE P. WILSON

Publishers of Singular
Fiction, Poetry, Nonfiction, Translation, Drama and Graphic Books

Library and Archives Canada Cataloguing in Publication

Title: I do remember the fall / M.T. Kelly ; introduction by Stephen Williams ;
  drawings by Catherine P. Wilson.
Names: Kelly, M. T., author. I Williams, Stephen, 1949- writer of introduction.
Series: Exile classics ; no. 30.
Description: Series statement: The Exile classics series ; number 30 I Originally
  published: Toronto : Simon & Pierre, 1977.
Identifiers: Canadiana (print) 20190159146 I Canadiana (ebook) 20190159162 I
  ISBN 9781550968699 (softcover) I ISBN 9781550968705 (EPUB) I
  ISBN 9781550968712 (Kindle) I ISBN 9781550968729 (PDF)
Classification: LCC PS8571.E4477 I2 2019 I DDC C813/.54—dc23

We gratefully acknowledge the Canada Council for the Arts, the Government
of Canada, the Ontario Arts Council, and the Ontario Media Development
Corporation for their support toward our publishing activities.

Canadian sales representation:
The Canadian Manda Group
664 Annette Street, Toronto ON M6S 2C8
www.mandagroup.com 416 516 0911

North American and international distribution, and U.S. sales:
Independent Publishers Group, 814 North Franklin Street
Chicago IL 60610 www.ipgbook.com toll free: 1 800 888 4741

to my friends

INTRODUCTION

In this day and age when anybody who is nobody can publish anything they write – and do – the quality of the work of M.T. Kelly is a beacon to a bygone era when writers had to be able to catch the attention of professional editors and their publishers who were only interested in what they perceived to be quality writing – either fiction or non-fiction – with commercial potential.

Believe it or not, this bifurcated system of publishing is thriving today in a marketplace inundated with hundreds of thousands of self-published works, only the smallest percentage with any merit and fewer still ever read by anyone other than the writers' relatives. Success in publishing is still defined by writing ability, dexterity with language, story, quality, serious marketing, promotion and vigorous distribution. And real success remains as challenging as ever.

I have no idea whether the Wild West that is the world of modern publishing makes more worthy reading material more easily accessible than before but one thing for sure, the production of books is never going to revert to the old model.

M.T. Kelly's *I Do Remember the Fall* is a relic from the past and a window on a dramatically less politically correct era. However, it does not deserve to be thought of in that context nor should it be relegated to obscure backlists. As this new Exile edition proves, it's as readable, contemporary and outrageously funny as it was when it was first published in 1977.

I have known M.T. Kelly since the long-ago days when we were both aspiring writers, years before either of us had published a word. My subsequent scribblings* got me arrested (twice) over a decade that spanned the 1990s and early 2000s. His got him well-deserved prizes, respect and recognition. *I Do Remember the Fall* is an excellent example and it won the Books in Canada Best First Novel Award. And think of the fire in the belly such early success would light in a young writer. His third novel, *A Dream Like Mine* (1987), received the Governor General's Award for English Language Fiction, and was made into a fine, important, and still relevant movie called *Clearcut*.

I Do Remember the Fall is a coming-of-age story that begins in Eastern Canada, unfolds on the prairies, and ends with an entirely believable sense of exhaustion and transformation. Its protagonist, Randy Gogarty, leaves the Big City, rife with pubescent fantasies and preoccupations, takes a job at a newspaper in a far-flung prairie town in Saskatchewan, and emerges a mature young man ready to face the future. All the characters Kelly brings to life on the page he draws with a David Annesley-like precision and sense of caricature. When all is said and done, it's one of those cocoon-to-butterfly fables that rings absolutely true.

Stephen Williams
July 2019

---

* *Invisible Darkness: The Horrifying Case of Paul Bernardo and Karla Homolka*
  (Bantam Books, New York, 1997)
  Karla: A Pact with the Devil
  (Penguin Random House, Toronto, 2004)

CHAPTER ONE

Train rides. I mean, who do you *ever* meet on them? It's just Canada, and going across all that space, seeing the towns and mills and wishing you knew someone in them, knew each of their streets and places, and you do really, even looking down from a railway bridge, and wishing you loved someone in them.

Here I was on the CPR, in a compartment. Oh yes, a compartment. I've done the coach bit, and done it, and done it, and will do it again, but I had a compartment this time.

Fifteen minutes out of Toronto's Union Station I pulled a chicken leg out of my box lunch. Why wait? Only two days to go. We were passing the house where my grandmother had lived – bless her dead, immovable, fat-encrusted Victorian heart – and there was my mother, the present occupant, waving. Her stomach below the halter top and above the shorts jiggled in the sun like a flag. "Hi, Mom." I waved, "Bye, Mom." Poor little girl. Seeing the place go by, it was like I'd never moved at all, been anywhere, if you know what I mean, in my whole life, and these kinds of thoughts can make you sad.

Speaking of girls, however, I was reading Evelyn Waugh and dreaming of pale English girls and silver tea services. My trip went like that, dreaming of a softer sunlight with chicken grease on my chin, masturbating every hour or so and watching my balls in the chrome. The chrome reminded me of Thirties architecture, as did the fittings in my room.

The landscape of the south floated past, the yellow and grey and green that are its colours becoming wraith-like, humid, brooding as night slid in.

I tried not to notice the factories, all of them, I'm sure, full of dazed demented workers and all located on the flattest most unattractive land. They were miniature deserts with wire fences surrounding them and yellow drums stacked neatly inside the fences.

When the train went through woods there was mist and great flowers of trees. I was dizzy, dreaming, elated – and getting bored. This couldn't go on. I'm sensitive, so out I go into the corridor for a walk.

Sure enough, down the car, there's a girl sitting in her compartment. It's dim by now, and I can see white pants, and tanned ankles. She had big feet, but her ankles were nice all right. And she had lovely unwashed stringy sun-streaked blond hair. Sitting in there.

How did I get to meet her? I probably said something brilliant like, "Why don't you turn your light on?" or "Going to Vancouver?" Stuff like that can work if accompanied with a smile. I mean, I know people often want you to talk to them but it's hard.

I've had success meeting women, more than most. It isn't meeting them that's difficult. Usually I meet them in places like the subway or at parties where I scream over the voices of my friends and demand attention, certainly never travelling or in night-clubs. My approach is: "Hi, I'm articulate and harmless. I'm also funny."

Jean was her name, Jean from Pittsburgh. She'd been studying in Berkeley and San Francisco: Art. I don't know if it was all the fumes she'd been sniffing in her studies – her specialty was plastic and chemical art, you know, plating toothpicks with carcinogens and then scattering them on hot wet plastic – but the bridge of her nose was wide and flat. It could have been broken or else all the tissue had swelled and been eaten away by irritants. It made her conventional face a hatchet, much more character really, and she had this big wide mouth.

"Men never fall in love," Jean told me. "That's what my father said to me; men never fall in love."

"Tell me about the whores in San Francisco," I said. "I read this book about a pimp and how he controls his girls. They sell their bodies for love. They love and he doesn't. He who loves less is stronger, that sort of thing. Is that what your father meant? Ever seen any whores?"

"Well..." Jean didn't have a breathless voice, but nearly. She was quite dull. I mean she didn't give at all. I was too busy giving her everything she didn't ask for – loudly.

"These businessmen next door to me, you should see it, at eight in the morning they drive up in big cars and the girls meet them in evening gowns."

"Evening gowns?" I said.

"Evening gowns. In the morning." This must have seemed the height of perversion to her, an evening gown in the morning.

"What do the guys look like?"

"Businessmen," she said. The telegraphic style of conversation can get ridiculous sometimes.

"Fat, greasy, blue-jowled, eh?" I said.

"Short," she said.

"Do you like your boyfriend?" I asked. "You mentioned breaking off, at least I think you did."

"Well..."

"Don't commit yourself now," I said. "You don't have to tell me all this personal stuff. What's your father like?"

"He's a businessman."

"Is he short?"

"He drinks."

3

"We all do. Yes, I will share your wine." She had a bottle of lovely French white wine which dad had given her in Toronto for the trip, probably as he was telling her men didn't fall in love.

"How long does it take to get across the country?" Jean asked. "The trains in Canada are supposed to be the best way to travel. I'm heading south from Vancouver."

I wanted to talk about pimps and whores and alcohol, not the beauties of the Big Sur country, so I didn't encourage her to talk about her trip. I did explain about mine, however.

Elk Brain, Saskatchewan, was my destination. I was going out west to start my first job on a newspaper, *The Elk Brain Tribune*. Needless to say, I had made quite a mess of my life in Toronto, mostly living off the beneficent and intelligent and very kindly government, though I had worked as a business journalist for one of the largest publishing companies in Canada. Being fired from that place was like getting bounced out of a leper colony.

They'd had a training program and I had been training longer than I should have been. It was no fault of mine really, getting stuck. A mild recession had made openings rarer than usual that year. Well, I hacked it for four months but after that it was Valium and beer at noon.

My boss, the copy editor, was a woman who'd worked her way up from 20 years on a provincial paper to this job. She'd been a city editor, which I've come to know is no big deal, believe me. Twenty years of rewriting everyone's copy and exposure to Canadian Press style hadn't given her tolerance for other kinds of writing, much less ways of thinking. She started writing memos to all of us "editorial assistants" for spending too much time in the washroom.

Our big treat used to come at the end of the day when she'd pull her *Globe and Mail* out. We were supposed to read it every day, part of the job you know, being a professional. Out would come the

Globe at quarter-to-five and we'd all have a "talk." Jesus! Recreation time in the sweatshop. It was about as relaxed as when the funeral director tells you how to lift the coffin. Her smile, she performed a very formal facial movement she thought of as her smile, had all the hilarity of cancer. This accordion-like retreat of flesh back from her buck teeth was really self-congratulation – see, folks, I'm interacting and surviving in a big company, it said.

The woman didn't have a clue other people existed, I'm sure of it. Her human relations had all the reality of a pulp article, the kind of desperate delight that things are okay – they're okay! – you get in a *Reader's Digest* feature on "How to Control Necrophilia in Your Husband." Everything, everyone, was an article to her.

Pronouncing the words "upper management" seemed to be her major sexual thrill. She'd fawn and beam her buck-toothed grin. The dandruff would light up inside her hairnet.

Her husband certainly didn't have much to do with sex. She "loved" to travel and wrote for *Canadian Geographic*, and on one of her trips she had married her Filipino guide. He came to Toronto with her and I heard hints that his family was on the way: 150 uncles and brothers and sisters and cousin-brothers and great-aunts and parents and godparents. Old Wally didn't have it all straight – her husband's name was Wally – but they *were* coming over. The family sounded like it automatically doubled in size at the mention of Canada.

Her name was "the Hornet." We call her the Hornet because her girdled legs made the sound of an insect's wings when she walked.

Our main job under the Hornet was writing new product blurbs. These were really free advertising for the manufacturers the business magazines were aimed at; great magazines like: *Canadian Sump Pump; Tree Chopper, The Magazine of The Canadian Forest*

Industry; Canadian Civic Sewage; Beat Botulism, A Magazine for Restaurateurs.

Now, the Hornet's memos got to me. As a defiance I used to have regular sessions in the can, stoned out of my mind after lunch, whacking off to save my soul. I had to listen to hear the door creak, which meant someone was coming. Then I'd control my breathing, sometimes I'd even whistle, and pretend I was taking a shit or cleaning my glasses in the sane little cubicle.

Never whack off in your company office before noon. All the boys are in washing their hands, getting ready to be let out. It's a regular parade. Middle mornings and the quiet part of the afternoons are best.

Believe me, I'm an expert on the subject. I've beaten off 32,000 feet in the sky, in mid-Atlantic, in trains, in buses – even while driving. Because of all this activity I've got the bladder control of a neurotic, and kidneys the size of lima beans.

The Hornet wasn't concerned about my kidneys. Even without my sessions I like a break, just going for a drink of water. But that was being away from your desk, *verboten*. It got to the point where it was either her or me.

It was me. But I didn't go quietly. I was the first person in company history to make a scene.

"Sit down," I said to her. She was trying to ignore me by putting papers away. Very proud of her back files she was – you never know when they might come in handy. All that newsprint she stored had the smell of dirty laundry.

"Sit down," I said. "I've listened to you for eight months, now it's your turn."

She was getting red.

"One doesn't talk to you, madame, one punctuates. So just listen for a moment. You, madame, are a punctilious tyrant. You better look the word up, it has more than one syllable…" I went on a bit, not too long, then ran up eight floors to tell the only other "human being" in the company the news. Running down the aisles to his cubicle I made noise, and I don't think the other human being has ever forgiven me. It may have hurt his career, you see. He was the kind of guy who got married because he was afraid he was going bald. He mentioned it to me beside the coffee truck one day and a few months later he was married. He became very successful.

This kind of behaviour, while satisfying certain of the emotions – I wanted to put the Hornet's fallopian tubes in a linotype machine and watch her unravel across the office – isn't good for a career. Later, a personnel man said to me: "Mr. Gogarty, you didn't burn your bridges, you blew them up."

But someone had finally hired me! Granted, it was one of the cheapest multinational corporations going, founded by a goggle-eyed Canadian; spread across the earth; making sure whatever quivering, feeble quality it found in the newspapers it took over was immediately crushed beneath the weight of ads from other corporations. But they had hired me. Although they were so cheap I had to pay my own way to Elk Brain.

"Yes," I said to Jean. "I'm a journalist so I can always get work, travel."

"I'd like to get into something like that," she said. "I'm getting disillusioned with the art scene, it's so phony."

"Yes, I can always get a job."

It's a compulsion with me to say things like that. I'm always going around telling people I can get a job. Hah! The only travelling expense I ever had was bus fare to go to Don Mills and interview a comptroller. It was a personality piece. He was big on golf.

An idea I have – and it's not only an excuse for my own failures – is that girls like identities. They go to bed with young lawyers, med students, salesmen, preferably musicians, not people. You are what you do, so I take "journalist." What I am is a lower middle-class loser with a mediocre BA and a love of poetry.

This identity stuff is true. In Ottawa, for instance, you have to be AT1 (Administrative Trainee, First Grade) to get people to talk to you. I was visiting Ottawa once and my hosts were going to put me up in the basement. Then they heard me mention I knew someone in the Privy Council. A collective orgasm took place: I was offered wine and dinner, even one of their own beds. That city makes 14th-century Florence seem positively egalitarian.

"Art is cheapened by the dealers in New York," I said to Jean. "And those critics. Clement Greenberg! Anti-human scum. Fuckin' Americans."

By this time, of course, the wine isn't doing me any harm, rolling along in the dusk, still no lights on in the dim steel cabin, her curled up with those luscious big feet, knotted and gnarled and bunioned and beautiful, tucked under the white pants. There were stains around her cuffs like charcoal, her thongs hung from between her toes like banana leaves.

Jean, sweet thing, didn't seem to notice my anger. All I was praying now was that someone else wouldn't come along and join us. I could sense Jean was friendly enough at this stage to be all for that sort of thing. I slid her cabin door shut. Too many people had been going back and forth in the corridor and looking in. It was the way I'd found her.

"You wouldn't believe it," she said. "You have to know the right dealers."

"I believe it."

"You have to know the right dealers."

"Maybe you could expand on that," I said.

"It's who you know."

"Right. So they can fit your masterpiece into the lobby of the World Trade Centre. Tell me, why does art fit in so well with those places? Corporate art. And what's wrong with literary subjects?" The questions were stolen but they were good ones and I wanted to know.

Jean shrugged. She told me about her boyfriend who was an art student as well; how she wanted to leave him but missed him.

"What's he look like?" I asked. I'm always interested in what people look like. Myself, I'm medium height, a little stocky, with bright blue eyes behind steel-rimmed glasses and a vigorous cropped beard. My hair is blondish, and I'm worried about growing a bald spot. I'd like to wear jewellery, but I don't. There's something "intelligent" about me that reminds people of the high school suck, sissy, you know, the poor fucker who could put a sentence together in history class. My yearbook entry read, "Those questions in Room 28!" Big joke. The other students were about as interested as cholera victims would be in more swamp water.

This "intelligent" quality I worry about makes people think me funny, odd. One damn broad called me effeminate, though she admitted later it was the wrong word. She meant sensitive. I've never stopped resenting her. I gesture a lot, and I like corduroy.

Jean's boyfriend on the other hand was tall, with thick black hair, a pencil thin moustache and Moroccan sandals. Need I say more. The details weren't hard to get out of her.

I could see the two of them together, eating health food and oranges for breakfast, spitting the seeds into each other's saucers. Real homey, both wearing cut-off shorts and getting ready to go off down the street to a tough day in the art school coffee shop. They probably clipped each other's toenails, not to be scorned as an act of love if they both wore sandals all day in a city.

The two of them would have tanned legs and basket-weave placemats, boredom and dissatisfaction and too much of each other every night. There wouldn't be an excess of conversation in their relationship, but there'd be a lot of "look what I made today" pointy-tongued lip-licking cuteness on her part. Smiling. Sunlight. I know he was the silent type. I wasn't jealous at all, not of their little apartment, not old 10-years-in-a-furnished-room Randy Gogarty, not at all. Intellectually I knew I'd be up the wall in two days living like that, intellectually.

Now the conversation wasn't exactly rollin' along at this point. I learned Jean was going back to live with the guy.

"Tell me about your father," I said. The smoke blackened, steel mill skies of Pittsburgh beckoned. "What do your parents think of your art?"

"Oh, they like it."

"None of this 'get a job' stuff, eh?"

"No. If I'm happy at it then it's all right with them."

I could see the old prick when he got drunk, leering, looming close to her with his monstrous out-of-focus sentimentality, the sacks under his eyes moist: "Ass long ass you're happy, baby, then it's all right, okay? Ass long ass you're happy..." *ad infinitum* as only drunks can go on.

"What is your dad like?" He was starting to fascinate me with his "men don't fall in love" and "my little girl" world view. If I couldn't talk about whores and pimps I'd talk about a happily married man with the same philosophy. "What do men do if they don't fall in love?"

"He drinks."

"Oh." I thought we'd established that.

"He's built a business himself and now that he's about to retire he has nothing to do," Jean said. "My mother's great though, and she's very busy. She's really great, a great person."

"Does she drink?"

10

"A little. She'll come home and have a gin and tonic."

"Dad has lots of gin and tonics, eh?"

"Bourbon and water. He usually has a couple before dinner. Then he watches TV. Mother tries to keep him busy and she's doing a good job of it. It was his idea to bring us all up to Toronto, and his idea about the train trip."

"Are you sure Mommy didn't plant it?"

"No!" She was getting irritated.

"Why didn't your parents come with you?"

"They live in Pittsburgh!"

"Oh right." I didn't say sorry. "What else does your dad do?" I doubted he did very much.

"He has a slight heart condition. Mother's so active. He started out with very little."

"What business is he in?"

"Asphalt; he paves things."

"Do you think men fall in love, Jean? I mean, I've seen men sick over women."

"In a way. But it's different."

"How?" My favourite topic is this power relationship stuff. I always talk about it, especially to strangers, and especially if they're women.

"Hmmmmmmm," she said, looking out the window. Not that there was much to see, the window a sheet of Vitralite black.

"Women don't like guys who beg. Right?"

"Right."

Boy, was she distracted, her broken face etched clean as a child's in the feeble light, her tan yellowing.

Should I go back and talk about Dad? He at least had something to do with the topic with which I was concerned. But look where talking about Dad had led us, the bourbon-drinking,

TV-watching bastard. Might as well blame him for the failure of our conversation.

"What's your house like?"

Nothing. I hadn't even asked which house.

"Do you think I'd get along in the States?" I said. "As you can see, I'm glib and aggressive."

"Yes."

Well, that was something. She thought me a potential success. But if I'm such a potential success how come I found myself saying, "Well, I guess I better be going now."

As I stood up I felt I was a giant, a raw-boned prognathous monster leaning over a little girl in a crinoline. A friendly giant of course. And like all sympathetic hunchbacks I know when I'm not wanted. Still...

"Do you want to talk a little longer?" I asked.

"No. Really. I'm pretty tired, I think I'll go to bed."

A joke like "that's what I had in mind" would have been disastrous, right?

"That's what I had in mind."

Nothing.

"Ha, ha," I said.

"Ummmmmm," she said and smiled, privately. I found myself sliding open her door and being slid out.

"Jean, I would like to talk, you know what I mean?"

She smiled a small distant smile, friendly and wistful, but the smile was directed at someone else, miles away. I wasn't there.

Back in my own cabin I got desperate. I started to hum "When you ain't got nothin' you got nothin' to lose." Typical I should sing something by a wizened rich, bitter little American at a time like this. And those beautiful mindless silver girls of Evelyn Waugh weren't enough, not for the night. Back I went.

"Jean, Jean."

No reply.

"Jean." The corridor had been darkened for the night. I stood there. Everyone was in bed and the train was swaying its slow way northward, lurching around bends. The forest, I knew, was close to the tracks, and it seemed to press through the aluminum sides of the Pullman, spruce black on a starless night, a large darkness, fainter above the trees, comforting.

The next day I went back, proud man that I am. Her door was shut tight, its blank face very final. I'd probably forced her to hole up for the whole trip. That's what I like about travelling, you really get to know people.

Now, I like to be friendly. There I am in the snack bar having a bite. I'd just come back from a try at Jean's closed door. She hadn't answered. I was feeling a little shaky, even though I didn't have a hangover. Along with this frailness was some delight, and not the delight of a wave of nausea in an hour or two, alcohol style. No, it was the feeling you get after a long romance you break off, a sense of possibilities. In other words, I was over Jean, Jean sitting back there locked up like she was some kind of 40-year-old hiding from the day until it was cocktail hour. That's how I saw her.

After an experience like that, especially one you feel good about, you tend to indulge yourself, "be good to yourself" as the therapists and women's magazines say. I was really being good to myself. You know the attitude, don't be extravagant, be healthy; so I order a healthy cholesterol-ridden tasteless omelette. Pork fat was what I fancied.

Once, I lived in a co-op with this moron who'd spent so many years in therapy, where they'd taught him to be good to himself, that he became the most petty, pampered, self-concerned selfish man I'd ever met. Believe me, living with a six-foot foetus like him had taught me the inherent dangers in being good to yourself. That's why when this old man comes up and says, "May I join you, sir?" and sits down without waiting for an answer, I deliberately didn't notice.

"Certainly."

I didn't think of the guy as a hair shirt I had to put up with or anything. I do know I tried to like him immediately. He was American, with one of those plaid shirts old men or little boys wear, and the lenses of his glasses were thick.

"Ah'll have some apple pie and ice cream," he said to the waiter. "That'd be just right about now."

Poor old guy, I thought, trying to pass off as courtliness something aggressive in his manner and gestures, a wide flabbiness and loose insensitivity to all but himself and what he was saying.

"Ah love trains," he said. "Ah'm sure AMTRAK in the States is making a mistake by running trains so fast. They should go slow like your Canadian trains. This here is my last trip, of course. Ah yes. Would you believe Ah'm 72, a volunteer fireman in Vermont…"

At this point, if he was wanting me to feel a little sorry for him, he was succeeding. I was softening on Americans, old cracker barrel Vermont, all those people who were nice in spite of being victimized by General Motors. I was almost starting to write a short story in my head called "Dad."

"…and Ah'm a Republican," he continued. "Yep, have been for 42 years."

I sort of wished he was disillusioned with politics.

"Ah'm going north to Alaska. As a matter of fact Ah have a suitcase of trinkets for the Eskimo children in my cabin. Would you like to come and see them? To trade, you know, beads. And my rifle. Ah might do a little huntin'. Game's gone down my way, though Ah still get a squirrel or stray dog or two. Damn strays!"

"No, thanks."

"This apple pie hits the spot. Ah'm a vegetarian, 'cause it says in the Bible and my religion…"

"Trains are capable of going at high speeds," I said quickly. I didn't want him to get into religion. He wasn't a Jehovah's Witness, they eat meat. But I knew whatever he was had Evangel in the title.

"Don't ask me about it!" he snapped. "Read about it yourself, find out about it yourself."

What! Who'd asked him anything?

"When Ah was a boy," (suddenly he was expansive), "Ah was curious. So Ah read the biography of Ford and Rockefeller." He leaned over and ordered, "You read that!"

"What does this have to do with trains?" I asked in all innocence.

"Find out yourself."

"Wait a minute," I said.

"Ah wouldn't talk to a Democrat. Ah hear there's a communist government in this here Saskatchewan, and that's unhealthy."

"You don't have to get off the train," I said. "We're only passing through. Anyway, they're not communist. They're called the NDP, sort of social democrats."

"Ah wouldn't talk to a Democrat."

"WELL, WHAT ABOUT KENT STATE?" I shouted. I think I was getting hysterical. "The NDP don't go around shooting people."

"Ah was in the militia during the war. 'Course Ah wanted to go overseas but had flat feet. Well, one night…"

"What?"

"…we drove a tank through town. Bob, the local police constable, knew us. 'Yes sir,' he said to Lieutenant Hargrave. Them West Point fellas don't fool around." The old man chuckled with delight at his intimacy with all this authority. "But look here. Have we had any trouble since Kent State? Look how quiet it's been."

"Are you kidding?"

"Shoot them."

"We're not as violent as you," I said to this lonely old man who was evil. "We're not violent." I wanted to unplug the resuscitator he'd soon be on after this last vacation for which he'd saved his pennies. "We're not violent," as I wanted to smash his face, break those glasses and watch him fumble and feel for them before I shot him. Oh yes, I thought of shooting him in those polluted Vermont woods just as he came out of his mobile home. He'd fall amidst the polyethylene petunias and his plaid shirt would catch on the tin steps.

This man made me gasp. A sense of disbelief that was real hatred jumped from my body against his face. I was hollow. All the rationalizations about it being worthless to argue with people like him, about not being able to change anybody's mind, were doing me no good.

I had to leave, and I left without speaking. The closest I came to real violence was that I failed to excuse myself as I got up. I'd like to say my omelette was uneaten, but I'd finished those blank eggs.

"Now, would you have some black coffee?" he said to the bus boy as I walked away. "That'd be just right."

I hadn't heard the last of the old prick. Later on, in the dome car, old Jake, or whatever his name was, sat a few seats ahead of me. I couldn't resist punishing myself by overhearing.

He'd met another political theorist, a lady, a Canadian. You could tell she was Canadian because her accent wasn't as prepubescent as many geriatric American women, and her hair wasn't piled quite as high. She was going to Vancouver to visit her daughter. Fascinating stuff. This genius had sent a meatball to the

Minister of Corporate and Consumer Affairs when she thought the price of meat had risen so high it was," Ridiculous."

Jake wasn't listening. He was telling the story about driving the tank down Main Street. The two of them were chewing away, clicking dentures until finally he persuaded her to go to his cabin and look at his trinkets and rifle. Ah, the joys of conquest. The old chick had on corrective hot pants and preceded Jake down the aisle. He followed, proper and erect, chest out, his thick glasses moony with a blank walleyed stare. It was the last I saw of him.

The trip changed completely for me that night in Winnipeg. We stopped to change crews and I got off to walk around. The stuffy suspension of mid-journey was over now; soon we'd be in Elk Brain. My fellow passengers and I wouldn't nod at each other, we wouldn't have to be aware of each other anymore.

The wind was cold on the platform, coming from far away, speaking of something pure and empty. As the men refuelled the diesel, they talked to me and moved massive hoses around. They wore rubber gloves. The engineer said I should have made myself known in Dryden, I could have ridden in the cab.

Trains fascinate me. One of the best asexual ways to get to sleep at night is to imagine yourself in the companionway of a diesel engine, the bulbs small and dim. It's brown and gold and grey where you are and black outside. Where you are is oily and dim and cozy. Up front the cab is lit by green instrument lights and you hammer through the night.

Another of my favourites, sweet and close and grave-like, is to imagine myself in the hull of a freighter during a storm. The storm is above and the ocean – one's bunk is always below the water line – is only inches away, separated by the hull's plate. Out beyond this steel you can touch as you roll over is black, black, the ocean.

The prairie, what I saw of it that night, was an ocean of land. Tiny blue lights shone in a distance I'd never experienced. The prairie, at its best, is purple in times of change; its thin colour was to be the one constant of my trip.

CHAPTER TWO

Elk Brain at 5 a.m. isn't welcoming. I'll blame it on the dawn, a damp grey that fairly bludgeoned you with its inevitability; you knew it'd be there tomorrow, and the next day, day after day. There was no surprise in it.

CP isn't fond of passenger business and the great station was a wreck. The only thing that'd been replaced in 30 years was a poster reminding snowmobilers to beware of fast freights.

The local taxicab office was located in the building. Heaven knows how the skinny old woman dispatcher could see anything. One jaundiced light bulb lit the empty office. She'd been up all night, and up all night for years. Her face was as grey and unhealthy as the morning. She radioed a cab.

"Ironwood Hotel," I said to the driver. The publisher of the paper had asked me if I wanted him to arrange a hotel for me. He had. I was paying for it myself, though he'd paid for the phone call that told me I was paying for it myself.

We drove up Main, one of the first "Main Streets" I'd been on. Where was the beautiful sensitive dissatisfied wife of one of the locals that I was going to have an affair with? She'd walked these streets. They were touched by her presence. I'd take her away from all this.

"Nice day," I said to the taxi driver. I hoped he thought I knew where I was going.

He didn't answer. He knew I didn't know where I was going.

Main was wider than anything in the east, discounting 20-lane expressways. There were lots of places for cars to park diagonally.

All the buildings looked like furniture stores because of their half-broken electric signs. I noticed a restaurant call The Polynesian Village.

The room that had been reserved for me at the Ironwood wasn't ready. It was $20 a day. I made do with a cheaper one, quite happily, and went to sleep. The bedspread was musty, the sheets starchy, and I was dizzy and foul-mouthed with fatigue. But when I awoke at about nine, oily and sour, prairie sun was pouring through my window. I walked over and looked out at a corrugated iron roof, the local hockey rink. There was the sound of traffic. Life in the 20th century. I washed and went off to work.

Work, can you believe it? A job's a rare and wonderful commodity these days. At least a job that you think means something, even if it doesn't.

There I was out on the street, and I was glad. There I was: Horatio Alger in Elk Brain; H.L. Mencken at his first paper in the Midwest; Hemingway at the *Kansas City Star*; Randy Gogarty *employed* in a new place, in different sunlight, in a different part of the world.

Politely and joyously I asked a policeman where the *Tribune* was – I could see its flaking black sign, but I wanted to open my mouth – and off I went.

The *Tribune* Building was sparse inside to say the least, the same institutional mint as my railway compartment or a washroom. The switchboard and old Marge, the switchboard operator, were mahogany.

"Mr. Pounder," Marge called back into an empty space behind her, "there's a Mr. Gogarty to see you."

From around a far wall, at the end of the steel Want Ad desks, Big Bill "just call me Bill" Pounder appeared, smiling his cherub's smile. He was big all right, my new boss, the publisher of the *Elk*

Brain Tribune, with well-formed wet lips and a sweet empty baby's smile. There was a cigar in his hand, his clothes were clean, and his pants slung low. A fold of his pants crept over his belt so you could see the lining, fresh from the cleaners, but tea stained all the same. His feet were neat and deft and his hair oil shone.

"Hi," he said, "we didn't expect you till Monday."

"Oh, I thought..."

"Nice trip? Come on into the office. I'll get Nick. OH NICK," he yelled back into the same empty space Marge had.

"Sit down, sit down," Bill said once we were in his office. I'd persist in calling him Mr. Pounder for the next few days, heaven knows why. Sycophant that I am, I guess my mother taught me well. She'd always told me as a kid that calling people "Sir" and by their last names was a way to get grown-ups to like you. Jesus, no wonder I'm a masochist. I don't want to please too badly.

Nick showed up, Nick Zudwicki, the editor. He had the same hairstyle as Bill, long on the sides, combed back. Thick, I might add, not being jealous. His face was Slavic, one of those Hungarian freedom fighter faces, bruised by some sort of inferiority he felt in his heritage, and rabidly capitalistic.

"This is our editor, Nick Zudwicki," Bill said settling back. "He'll take care of you. When do you want him to start, Nick?"

"Monday."

"Monday," confirmed Bill.

Monday! I thought. This was Thursday. But I didn't have time to think. Nick turned and started to leave the room. Wait a minute! Nick stopped. Bill was supposed to be settling back. Was this all? No, thank God. I'd almost felt for a moment there that I wasn't important.

Bill continued, "You'll start Monday as city hall reporter. Had some experience, eh?" He shook his head quickly to the side as if he was about to say goddamn, or goddamn right, or goddamn she's a bitch. The whole thing about this gesture, however, was that you said nothing. I'd seen this salute of acknowledgement and accord before. It was rural and supposed to be friendly. Bill was not rural. At least he hadn't spent much time in the outdoors in the last 20 years, and the friendliness was unequivocally on his terms.

"By the way, there's a little get together Saturday night at Nick's house. I want to talk to you staffers. There might be some labour trouble, nothing serious. He'll give you the address. Bye."

What was I going to do in Elk Brain till Monday? Nick hadn't moved and he hadn't said a word. That meant he was a professional, I guess. He didn't waste words. Now he moved quickly, looking efficient in a workaholic way, pasty face, pens in his pockets, sleeves rolled up, shirt none too fresh, a real editor. But yes, he was saying something. He pointed to an empty bird cage in Bill's office and said, "That's where he gets his ideas – Bird Brain."

He was joking with me, he liked me! Ah, the staff got on well. I'll grab at any straw.

We got outside the office and Nick said goodbye to me, showing me the Want Ad desk in case I needed to look for a room.

What did I do till the staff party?

SCREEEAMMM! – Not much.

I wrote postcards in my hotel room, feeling very busy, for about 15 minutes. Then I began to climb the wall.

I found my room – $45 a month, bed, stove and plugged sink. I went to the movies, choosing *Enter the Dragon* instead of *Digby, the Biggest Dog in the World*. *Digby* had been held over and looked like it was due for a long stay. The drive-in was out since I had no car, and I didn't bowl. So I sampled the bars.

Let me tell you about the bars. They were to play a central part in my life in Elk Brain.

Everybody was too big in them. There was an air force base and a provincial hospital for the retarded near the town (you had to say "eh" a lot) and I couldn't tell if the large customers I noticed were air force pilots or knuckle-head attendants. Their wrists hung out of their windbreakers, and they looked like they'd had too many vitamins as kids. Maybe they were all off-duty Mounties, you'd think so from the haircuts. Their displacement of space was insensitive, if you know what I mean. The girls, though smaller, also had this overgrown quality. Big legs in tight jeans with flat asses. Everyone's face showed they'd been exposed to dry air, and dust came out of the jeans when they were slapped.

But I'm being slightly unfair. The clientele just described frequented the Ironwood, and it catered more to high school kids. There was also the Wagon Wheel.

The Wagon Wheel was the singles bar of Elk Brain. It was darker and cooler than the Ironwood, less a barn, and the people were older, less exuberantly alcoholic. I met Audrey there. She was 40, a waitress in white go-go boots, and she spoke to me. As a result, I wanted to go home with her.

Audrey thought I was kidding. I wasn't. But I didn't mind her refusal. We had many more pleasant conversations after that, though they never came to anything. I'm glad because I found out later her son was an 18-year-old psychopath who didn't appreciate his mother's lovers.

There were other bars: The Horsehoof, a country music place with a reputation for fights. Near the Horsehoof was a depressing row of hotels. This street was frequented by Indians and pensioners. The Ironwood and the Wagon Wheel became my bases of operation.

My trips between hotels were interrupted by the Saturday night get together.

Nick's house was a quiet little bungalow on one of Elk Brain's side streets. I don't know what I expected from an editor, maybe a hobby of collecting first editions of Oscar Wilde in his off moments, but this place was too ordinary. I thought, he could've been a foreman at Kodak or something, like my uncle Jack.

I always head for the kitchen at parties. It's not to talk to the boys talking hockey in the kitchen. They've been there since high school, they never move. No, I head for the kitchen to open bottles.

The kitchen at Nick's was gleaming. A pot of coffee perked on the bright stove, and there were trays of canapés on the table. These were not the signs of a gutter-rolling drunk. I began to think I didn't want to meet Nick's wife.

It was Nick who had opened the front door, let me in, and now stood about as I opened my beer. A real host. He wasn't saying much, just "Okay, Randy?" after I cracked one.

"Okay, Nick."

I was led to the living room. Nick still walked quickly, but before he turned for me to follow he smiled fleetingly, almost wistfully. It seemed friendly. Maybe this'd turn out to be a good party.

All the staffers, except, of course, the real men talking hockey in the kitchen, were sitting around – quietly. They weren't quiet, they were dead. The pall my entrance increased didn't give me confidence. I was sure I had heard murmuring before I came in. Now all was silence. NO! Someone was secretly breathing through their mouth. I could hear it.

"Everybody. This is Randy Gogarty," Nick said, "our new city hall reporter." Then he began to list off a bunch of names. "Al, Eli, Bauxtrom, Barbara, I'll go clockwise..."

Who cares, I thought, nodding and smiling.

"...Tinkus, you've met Marge, Sid, Jerry and Jack, Angelo, Jim Chan, Iris, Harold."

One by one they smiled, each face breaking into a slit-eyed grin as their name was mentioned, pop, pop, pop around the room. I didn't see Big Bill anywhere.

"I'm sure you'll forget these names," Nick said. "Just do your best. Ha ha."

"Ha ha," I said, and headed for blond Barbara. There was a space beside her on the couch.

"Hi," she said, keeping her voice down, a narrow-shouldered, short-haired little thing. "I'm Barbara Birdwell, the women's editor, and this is Tinkus Dixford, our comptroller." Barb's voice was so gooey with delight and cuteness its pitch, even as she whispered, was almost a shriek.

Tinkus leaned forward. "Hello," he said and pulled out a chocolate bar. Slowly, he bit into it. It was obviously his one social pleasure. Each jowl, they weighed about 10 pounds each, collected and fell, collected and fell. Tinkus concentrated on his pleasure.

He's fuckin' mad, I thought. Tinkus had one of those looks, immensely pleased with himself, that I've never seen outside an institution.

"Tinkus is a bachelor, you see," Barb said.

"Oh," I said. I guess that was supposed to explain it.

"He's been with the paper 20 years."

"Oh. I see."

Just to confirm things Tinkus joined in. "I like parties. But there's a good show on TV tonight. *Mary Tyler Moore*. I watch it every Saturday."

Before Tinkus could continue Nick's wife showed up, from where I don't know, and announced food. "Just chips and dip and things, nothing much."

Tinkus got up immediately and lumbered after it.

"He's a bit strange, isn't he," I said to Barbara.

"Oh, I don't think he cooks very well for himself at home," Barbara said sympathetically. "Isn't Mary, Nick's wife, wonderful? She makes the best—"

"I haven't met her," I interrupted.

"Oh, you will. She's part of our group. Just some couples that do things together. Are you married, Randy?"

"No."

"Well, there's lots to do in Elk Brain," she enthused. "Curling and winter sports, bowling. Things really liven up in the fall – night classes at the high school, the drama club…"

"I'm interested in drama."

"That'd be Ollie Nestlebaum up at the high school. They're real good. They really have fun."

Tinkus returned. He was carrying a bowl of chips and a bottle of pop. Smiling, he sat down. His dentures grinned at us. He looked embalmed. Barb and I left him to it.

"I guess most of the people my age are married, eh?" I said to Barb. "The kids I saw at the Ironwood looked like they were in high school."

"Yes," she said. "A lot go to Calgary, or stay here and raise a family. I have a little girl. She looks just like me except she has curly hair. My husband, Dave, works out at the provincial hospital as a counsellor."

"Did you meet Dave in high school?"

"Uh-huh. People think we're twins."

From what I'd heard of these kinds of hospitals I didn't know what Dave did. How do you counsel a 40-year-old whose brain consists of the stem of his spinal column? No eyes, no head.

"Oh," I said pleasantly, a sweetish horror in my stomach. "What does Dave do in his spare time?"

"Last summer he and my father went camping."

"Do you ski?"

"No. But they built a hill outside of town," and off she went, insisting I'd like Elk Brain once I got to know people.

Mary Zudwicki came over to us in the middle of this catalogue. Nick was with her. He'd rolled his shirt sleeves up, so I guess he'd had a couple of drinks and was feeling at home.

"Well," Mary said, "enjoying Elk Brain?"

Before we could get into all that, Nick suggested I meet some of the other reporters. Mary beamed at me, waiting for an answer. Neither of them listened to the other. They got along well.

Nick spoke quickly, persistently but, strangely enough, sadly. This sadness had nothing to do with you, however. The impression came from his pasty colouring, his quiet manner, and the fact he barely moved his mouth when he talked. He looked tired, over-worked. It was like he was asking questions, politely, fairly, and cared about the answers, not who was giving them.

Mary, through her gleaming smile, was quiet and subdued, a good hostess beside her husband. Her smile, though unrelaxed, was softened by a kind of pastel in its flash, a hint it could tumble into a soft blank confusion. She had sharp features; their sharpness emphasized by a bouffant hairdo that left her face bare.

As I got up to go with Nick I could hear her, "Is that so?" to Barb's, "Real good!"

The party had livened up. You couldn't hear breathing or chewing any more; there was a pleasant little hum.

I was introduced to Zeke Hyba, cub reporter.

"You fellows'll have plenty to talk about," Nick said, and disappeared.

Zeke and I eyed one another. He was a small compact man in checkered pants. His glasses had slick racing frames and his hair was full, well-cut, brown and gold. There was a furtive hopeful look about Zeke, and anyone who hopes is fragile.

We said little, not knowing if we'd have to compete. Soon it came out that Zeke had only arrived in Elk Brain a couple of days ago, and that he also had had a hard time finding a room.

"We've got that in common," I said. "A shared washroom and cheap rent."

"Yes," Zeke said. "I share mine with two pensioners."

"From what I can tell I share mine with an amphetamine addicted brakeman on the CPR. He's 17 and just left home."

Oh, we had a lot in common Zeke and I. He had no fridge in his kitchen, but he had a kitchen. I had no kitchen but a sink and fridge in my room. Both sinks, it turned out, drained poorly and were small.

"Is Hyba a Ukrainian name?" I asked.

"Yes, but not the kind of Ukrainian you have in Toronto."

Zeke was sensitive about this, though not bitter, just as he was sensitive about the fact he'd dropped out of journalism at the University of Western Ontario.

Apparently, his kind of Ukrainian had received the poorer land in the prairies, north of Winnipeg. They were different.

What he said made sense. The Slavs at my high school in Toronto, the ones who sent their sons and daughters to Plast and Sum, or organizations with names that had a phlegm-like ring to them, were not the most liberal people in the world. They looked down on everybody, those sausage-eating Slavs, and only let their daughters date dentists of the same racial purity. I could understand Zeke's resentment. He'd thought once of becoming a Greek Orthodox priest; his brother was one. Just like the Irish. Somebody's always got to be a priest in those large families. Their farm was poor but solvent, and his parents despaired of Zeke ever holding a job.

"I didn't like London, Ontario," he said, "and the farms are so small down east." He lit a cigarette with nicotine-stained fingers.

"Compared to here they are." I said. "Western's a school I deliberately didn't go to. I knew I'd never meet anybody there."

As Zeke and I were about to continue Nick came back with another reporter.

"Fellas," he said, "this is Larry Brennen, the new sports editor. You'll all be starting Monday so you might as well get to know each other."

Nick left.

"What is this," I said before Larry had a chance to say a word, "a whole new staff? I heard I was going to be city hall reporter on Thursday, and I don't even know what it is."

"A high staff turnover," Larry said in answer to my question.

"Um," Zeke flicked his eyes away.

"What's this about labour trouble?" I went on. "Isn't Mr. Pounder supposed to give us some kind of talk or something?"

"Oh, Bill you mean," Larry said. "He isn't here yet."

Zeke backed up a step and looked at the floor.

I looked at Zeke, Zeke with his poverty-stricken parents and their high expectations. I knew we were thinking the same thing. My stepfather-in-common-law, my mother's boyfriend, in other words, "Uncle Mel," has similar views to Zeke's dad about the relationship between education and employment. I could see Zeke's dad shaking his head after having done all he could for the boy. Mel has called me "the Professor" for my six mostly unemployed years since university. "The *Professor* of nothin', har har." Mel's an alcoholic so it's easy to excuse him. My mother on the other hand hovers around, offering her savings so I can go to graduate school. Then maybe somebody'd hire me, she thinks, or at least I could go on and teach high school. They both make you feel guilty. I understood the consternation that crossed Zeke's features as it appeared that the job we hadn't started might not work out.

As I was musing, Larry Brennen took over.

"By God, this is insane, Yahoo. I remember when I was a disc jockey, before my lung collapsed – just call me One Lung Larry – well, I remember a situation like this when the technicians struck. By God, I supported them. To a man. You've got to be serious." Larry leaned closer and got serious, all five-foot-one of him. He closed one eye. "You've got to be serious about sticking to your union or not."

"Sticking to your union," I said.

"What union?" Zeke asked.

Larry didn't notice us, he was talking. "The technicians union at CBLM. I stuck and they stuck to a man. We supported each other."

"What happened?" Zeke and I asked together.

"I was fired. But it doesn't matter. Wherever I go in North America the technicians are with me."

"But you're not a technician?" Zeke and I were thinking along the same lines.

"I found another job in Muskeg, Alberta. It's a smaller town than Elk Brain, but I had sports and midnights and I was closer to Kitty. Kitty, that's my lady."

Larry twirled his handlebar moustache. He had this moustache, you see, and apparently Kitty's cunt juice made it grow. Or so he informed us. He demonstrated this by twirling it again and leering smugly into the air. His eyeballs rolled. Larry was a card, he said so himself.

"I'm a bit of a card," he said. "Jes-us! Look at that whale-backed fucker over there."

Zeke and I turned and understood Larry was indicating Tinkus. The *Tribune*'s comptroller was rolling across the living room toward the buffet table.

"How'd you like to take a pellet gun to that fucker's ass?" Larry asked.

"You're begging the question," I said.

"Jes-us! Imagine that bastard nude in the shower. He's probably got a pecker the size of a pea."

"Have you seen him nude?" Zeke said.

"I bet that hog-backed motherfucker hasn't ever seen squash court," said Larry, spitting the words out with a twinkle in his eye. This twinkle indicated that Larry fancied himself a bold gay devil. I was finding him quite pleasant. He had a toothy skeletal grin, as lacking in flesh as his body.

Larry described himself as wiry. He weighed 98 pounds. He told us a lot about himself – his cock size, how he could've been a jockey, his predilection for cunnilingus, the fact he didn't need much sleep. "Go for days," he said.

As if we hadn't clued in, Larry illustrated his sense of humour. "I was covering the football game, see, and the Riders made a 12-yard gain. 'That's 12 yards,' my buddy says to me. I points to the cheerleaders and says, 'Yeah, 12 yards of *cunt*.'" Larry told this joke out of the side of his mouth, making sure our hostess wouldn't hear. At the punchline he broke up, showing us the way he'd broke up at the game.

"I was a singer in a rock group," he said, "the Find Us out of Winnipeg." Larry did a dance step as he told us this, accompanied by a stage smile to prove he'd been an entertainer. He was bug-eyed with confidence and his need to be noticed. "All right!" he said.

The picture Larry created of himself wouldn't have been complete without the fact that his mother had cancer. He loved his mother and, although a man needed the occasional piece on the side, he loved Kitty.

To break this brief mood he went into another dance routine, this time pretending he was holding a microphone and smiling the way he'd smile at the girls. It was one of those self-consciously charming smiles, so obvious you can't believe it, that is always effective.

"You've gotta be a professional, eh?" Larry was giving advice. "I wanted those people to buy our album. I was never rude to anyone on the road."

I'm sure Larry was willing to tell us a great deal more – all my time in Elk Brain I found him a companion because he was willing to talk – but he was interrupted by the arrival of Big Bill Pounder.

Bill came up the hall accompanied by Nick. Almost laughing, gumming his cigar as it changed sides in his face, he pressed the flesh of the crowd. The crowd consisted of Zeke, Larry and I.

"Good to see you boys," he said and went on. He noticed us in the sense that he noticed we were there, a wet little flicker caught each of us, but that was all.

We heard Bill cry out "Mary!" when he got in the kitchen, but after that he seemed to disappear, and things went on much as before.

Bill wasn't a loud man, though he looked as if he should have been. He was too busy chuckling, beaming, congratulating you with his almost handsome fat man's face, to make any real noise. There was something very sweet and remote in the way Bill looked at you. Oh, he could get serious all right, but the next morning all would be well, and his cheeks would colour with puckers and dimples. "Hi there."

Larry, who as I said had a habit of crunching his face up in a practiced smile, was mainly conscious of his ability to smile like that, and he looked at you. Bill saw you but he didn't look at you.

We were being called into the living room for the talk. "Every-body, everybody," Mary was saying, "could you come in here for a minute." She sounded like some relative at a second-rate wedding demanding quiet before the toast to the bride.

The party crowded in. Barbara Birdwell got up and moved over to where we were because she didn't want to sit at Bill's back. The speaker of the hour was facing us. Probably Birdwell didn't want to sit while her boss was standing. Tinkus sat, an insane delight on his face as his innards assured him he was gaining weight.

"Well, everybody," Bill began originally, shaking the ash off his cigar with transparent chagrin, "as you know..."

"We don't know anything," Larry piped up. "Could you give us a little background."

This was not the way to win the boss's heart, I thought.

"I was about to get to that." Bill answered with respect, as if he was actually entertaining Larry's question, and not, as he should have been, marking him for demotion. "The union's been without a contract for six months."

"What union?" Larry asked. The whole room was hushed and angry with him; Bill receptive. It was disconcerting.

"The typographical union," Bill said, "So..."

Now we're supposed to have Bill droning on. But he was sur-prising. Just as his extroversion lay in his facial movements, his rhetorical style was silence. He said nothing, merely showed he'd not been offended by Larry's questions, and he didn't drone on. The room did. It hummed with a deferential little oil, sliding away from the subject of its concern like an undertaker after he's made a sale. Safely people smiled and moved to the buffet table. I guess getting a concrete fact like the name of the union made most of the guests more cautious than usual. Sharkskin suits with shiny seats flashed as salesmen with Methodist mouths munched white bread. Ginger ale sparkled in glasses. "Thank you, Mary, just a touch of rye," was the war cry.

"When does the wife swapping begin?" Larry said. "I'm a male slut."

"Ask the sports fans." I pointed to the boys who'd come out of the kitchen to hear Bill. They were heading back.

"How do you like Elk Brain?" Barb had joined the conversation. Her question was directed at Zeke. In order to avoid hearing more of this I paid attention to the press around me. Combined with Mary's mustard carpet and the beige walls it made me feel I was going to choke. Everyone's breath seemed to reek of coffee and cookies.

As I tried to watch Birdwell's mouth without listening to her just like women's libbers hate, a fat woman pressed her rump against me.

I caught a whiff of perfume and glanced at Barb's muscly legs in dark tights. No, it couldn't have been her perfume. It must have emerged from the vicinity of the rump behind me. It was hyacinth, a smell you'd get in a mausoleum with piped-in organ music.

Christ, Brennen was cupping Birdwell's ass! He'd snuck behind her as she was chatting to Zeke. She didn't notice, at least I hoped she did and was pretending not to, while Larry manipulated the tweeded lobes – she had a tweed skirt over her dark tights.

Why can't I accept what happens in this world? Girls who say no and mean yes; girls who say yes. Jehovah Witnesses who suck cock; Jehovah Witnesses who don't suck cock. Poetesses getting their teeth knocked out by their lovers. Accountants being gentle. Alcoholic secretaries "shitting" on those who are good to them and "balling" those who aren't. People who are self-destructive; people being so protective they have the personality of lichen. Men fucking girls and not wanting them any more; men not fucking girls and wanting them till they die, till they DIE, man. People lying to themselves on their death beds; people telling the truth. Jes-us! as Larry Brennen would say.

"So Daddy and Dave each took different sleeping bags. But they forgot the stove!" Barb was really getting into the story about her father's and husband's camping trip. Zeke looked at her rather ample waist, and Brennen burrowed in. I could see him concentrate as he tried to separate each cheek, his face blurring with lust. Barb arched her back slightly, offering her buttocks. I was sure Brennen was forcing a finger between the cheeks, like some European lucky enough to get behind a female tourist. Birdwell looked like she was listening to a lecture on cathedral architecture, though she was moving her mouth. Larry diddled away. Finally he got his finger in, and through two inches of tweed. He could've been gaffing a fish.

"Calgary's terribly expensive with the tourists and all, especially if you have to outfit there. I said to Dave when he phoned, 'Now don't you...' Oh, Mary," and Birdwell slipped by me. "I'll be back in a second," she said and smiled over her shoulder as she pushed through the crowd.

Had it happened? Larry still had his hands cupped in a parody of what he'd been doing. Then he made the predictable hourglass figure and went to get another drink. Zeke chuckled, or seemed to, but the soft sucking in of his breath betrayed him. The wrinkles round his eyes weren't laugh wrinkles, he was almost grimacing.

"Don't be bitter," I said.

Zeke shook his head. "Whew." Lines softened in his face, fine traces remained round his eyes.

Barb, if she knew what had happened, didn't let on. It was her last adventure before menopause.

CHAPTER THREE

Life in old Elk Brain didn't turn out so badly. I had my room, and a job, and no more staff parties to go to.

Every Monday I'd make a pot roast and eat it till Wednesday. Every Wednesday I'd make a fish chowder and eat it till Saturday. Belonging to a farmer's co-op made me feel like a Jeffersonian democrat, and the people I shopped with, although as middle-class and unlike the lords and ladies of Byzantium as supermarket shoppers anywhere, had the extra dimension of a weather-beaten look and an excuse for really narrow minds.

Three old brothers in the checkout line, apparently regulars every few months, lived on bread, flour, sugar, tea and Rice Krispies. I could imagine their kitchen, either filthy or scrubbed pale as water, and their diet and winters and hours. All the back-to-the-landers I know who want to dig with a stick for potatoes should see how some farmers really live. No matter though, those men loved their work.

I liked the overpriced cream pie at the co-op, and the thin light in the mornings walking to work. I liked the dust and the bleached quality to everything, the wind turning all lumber blue-grey as beech.

Nothing's perfect. I didn't like the way the wind and rain beat the cabbage patches black in people's backyards. The burned quality in faces didn't improve complexions. Everything I could get my hands on that was moist I read: the plays of Synge, Yeats, a travel book on Ireland call *The Gems She Wore*. The title appealed to me because I'm not romantic. Somewhere a girl's skin was translucent, she wasn't wearing cowboy boots, and her hair wasn't breaking from dryness.

Things could get a bit much at the hotels. In spite of my domestic little world, lying nude after supper, reading, as puff pastries baked in the oven and a saucepan of tea stewed on the stove, lying damp under the covers as humidity increased from the bubbling pot and the lovely lack of fresh air, in spite of all these gifts I did frequent the Ironwood Hotel. My usual was beer, pickled eggs, pickled sausage, pepperoni, beer nuts, and more beer. I talked to Audrey. Regardless of all this focusing on complexion, and Audrey had acne scars at 40, I invariably wanted her after 12 drafts. It was out of the question, of course, but I'd look at her heavy legs in her short skirt and want to tongue every crevice of cellulite. I met no other women and had time on my hands.

Time. How it used to get to me. Sundays were the worst. I had nothing to do but laundry. The overseer of the one laundromat in Elk Brain was a spotless old geezer in starched work clothes with a 400-pound wife and a plate of teeth he liked to click in disapproval. He'd bought the place to retire into and kept it pure as a bank vault and clean as a surgery. After this guy made sure my clothes weren't breaking his machines, and I wasn't using someone else's soap, I'd go over to the railway yards and watch the diesels, big freight engines.

I didn't always stand on the railroad platform freezing my ass off and brooding about symbols of escape like everyone has done in prairie novels since they've been written. What I did over at the CPR was savour the textures: the thick grease on the rails, the sound of the engines, the girders of the bridge, stark yet almost tender in the distance, west of where I stood. I liked it best when two units, moving slowly at the yard limit, were switched out to join a train. Their weight was a tangible presence.

An hour of this contemplation was enough. Then I'd retrieve my clothes. The laundry would be sickening after being outside, a steamy cloy that was overpowering. In spite of the frailty of the patron, and whatever fears or depression disadvantages accounted for his character, he enraged me. I was glad to get out of there and go home. Then it all came down. I mean, how much can you read, or write letters? One Sunday night, beside myself, I even went to Mass.

It was as disappointing and shallow as it ever was. Returning, I stood on the bridge I'd looked at in the afternoon. The night was cloudy above me: milky and vast and indifferent, but far more personal than the sour church and the embarrassing ritual that went on within.

But there was work. City hall reporters cover city council meetings. They didn't start me in this high position. First, I had to do a feature on the Boy Scout bottle drive. Proving satisfactory, that evening I went to council, accompanied by Nick.

Work. Nick introduced me around and then I started to take notes. I took them for four hours, and when we got back to the office Nick gently rejected every story idea I thought important, leaving me with his suggestions and his notes, and I typed till three. I had to be in again at eight. Positive reinforcement wasn't one of the tenets of Nick's creed, but he did say to me, "You tried, and that's what matters." I went to meetings myself after that, and worried, and did an adequate job.

This was the routine every Tuesday in Elk Brain, flood or famine. Of course, I got the afternoons off when I had a night assignment, and once I got used to council I didn't always burn the midnight oil, but my beat and my duty soon became a chore.

Part of my responsibility as city hall reporter included the labour scene. Needless to say it hadn't received much coverage; enlightened self-interest was a dangerous idea in our editorial room. When I suggested going to a Labour Council meeting, I met with some surprise. "We've tried. They don't want to give us any information." But my keenness was regarded as a good thing. There were no suspicions I wanted to be fair, and one empty Wednesday I found myself a spectator at a quorum of the EBFL, the Elk Brain Federation of Labour.

The union hall was a relatively new building in town, and the meeting rooms in its basement were much like modern high-school classrooms, windowless. I recognized a typesetter from the paper, Malcolm McSweeny, among those waiting for things to get started. It was a small turnout, a few men wearing coveralls or team jackets, their faces yellow with fatigue, sitting loosely on folding chairs. They weren't speaking to each other.

To my surprise Malcolm got up and went to the front of the room. He pulled a card table over in front of him to make a desk, sat down and started to write. No one had said a word.

Malcolm would glance up occasionally, lifting his eye over steel-rimmed spectacles like a New England stock-keeper, then go back to work. The way he hunched over what he was writing showed it was private.

McSweeny was an odd bird, a red-headed guy of 22 who almost looked normal. He had a square head, thick neck, those steel-rimmed glasses too small for his face, and friendly hair popping out of an open-necked shirt. His jeans always bore a red patch that said Calgary Export Ale. He must've had dozens of them. I hadn't realized Malcolm was big in labour affairs, though now I remembered I'd been referred to him once or twice to find out the dates of meetings. He'd cocked his head ironically and had given me the information, along with an invitation to come along.

Without being superior, Malcolm conveyed a sense of knowing something about you, and holding it back. His strange attractiveness must have been that you always wanted to find out what it was, or find out about him. Proselytizers for dangerous religions use this technique, they always approach one so knowingly.

My presence wasn't acknowledged, and I sat there a little uneasily, hoping I hadn't wasted my time in coming. At last Malcolm was joined at his card table by a prim older woman and a bald soft responsible-looking man who had to be the bookkeeper. He was.

The older woman started reading the minutes of the last Labour Council meeting, her lips grim, her voice very low. The present meeting had not been called to order; Malcolm kept writing; the bookkeeper shuffled some papers apologetically, hopefully.

Once the minutes had been completed a man stood up, a big man by the name of Nate Purgatoire, and demanded that the first order of business be my presence.

Malcolm condescended to look up.

"All I want to know is why the *Tribune* is sending someone over now?" Nate said. "By God, it's about time I say. But as the chairman knows, we have some business tonight that had best be handled *in camera*, if you take my meaning."

I wrote in my notebook while this was going on – the date and the initials of the labour federation.

Nate continued. "See. I don't like to be rude, but I don't want my name in the paper as someone who doesn't like reporters. From the coverage we've had I don't think it's right, and I don't think a man should stand for it. Twenty-five years in the union—"

Malcolm cut him off and droned, "Move for a vote that the meeting be held *in camera*, all in favour?"

Every hand in the place went up.

"Carried," Malcolm said.

"What's the big deal?" I asked. "If you haven't had coverage, I'll give you coverage. Why do you think I showed up? I'm not here to be dishonest."

"No press at this meeting," Malcolm said in a monotone that made your average bureaucrat's voice one of delight and wonder.

"Can I talk to you after?" I queried. I'll humiliate myself for people's trust. Fuck the news.

"Sure," Malcolm said. He was human again. "The lounge is down the hall. We're going to elect some officers; I'll give you their names."

The rest of the room was watching me indifferently. But if it was indifference, it was benign indifference. I shivered slightly as I walked out.

The main feature of the union centre lounge was a painting of the Bay of Naples on black velvet. It ran the length of one wall, covering the upper half. The ultraviolet lights that were hidden along the base of this mural had the desired effect: all the colours were as bright as the colours of an intestinal tract. Aside from these globs of incandescence, purple starlit night, mauve sea, pink ships and yellow houses, the lounge was a gloomy hole. To show the painting to best effect an effort had been made to keep all natural light out of the lounge, day and night. The effort had been successful. I sat at a table, barely able to make out where it was, and ordered a beer. There weren't many other people around: the jukebox silent, the dance floor empty.

"Have you got anything to eat?" I asked the waitress. "I haven't had any supper."

"Sure. Beer nuts, peanuts, pickled egg, pepperoni, and pickled sausage."

"Any hot dogs?" I'd noticed rollers for grilling them under the clock at the bar.

"We're out."

"Beer nuts, pickled egg and pepperoni," I ordered. "And you better bring me four more drafts."

I occupied myself in this familiar fashion until the meeting ended, and Malcolm came over to my table.

"Oh, here you are," he said. "We took a little longer than I thought. I wondered if you'd left."

"How long've you been?" I asked.

"Two hours."

"Oh. I hadn't noticed." I'm not sure I wasn't pouting.

"Jean," Malcolm called out. "Bring me a Calgary, will ?. Want another beer?" he said turning to me.

"Oh well, I..."

"Bring four."

That was the beginning. This buying of drinks! It was an intricate affair I was never to get quite used to, realizing all the time how one could be manipulated by someone constantly bullying you into drinking their beer, watching obligation accrue like items on a bill. The chief pastime at the union centre was ordering, then jockeying for the privilege of paying for those rounds.

Nate joined us, and the bookkeeper whose name was Wally Ellroy.

Nate leaned over, his huge forearms hairy as a spider's legs in the darkness, his face friendly, misshapen, conspiratorial. "What did you think of the EBFL?"

"I don't know anything about it."

Nate looked satisfied. No matter what I'd said he'd have looked satisfied. He was in on something I wasn't.

"It's good to have coverage," Wally said. "I hope you don't mind not being there. It's...you understand. We elected some officers you see, and there was a fuss about travelling expenses at the last convention. Nothing to really get upset..."

"Never mind, Wally," Malcolm cut in. "The new officers are." A list of names and positions followed.

"So what?" I said after taking the names down. "You know what kind of story this'll make, don't you? If it gets run. Buried on page three. Look. I'm not going to expose you if someone spent too much on breakfast at the last convention. I'm here because I want to be. This is a part of my beat that's been neglected. Nick didn't send me over here to spy on you by getting the names of your new executive. Believe it or not, I'm sympathetic to labour."

They believed me, pleased they were being paid attention to. I could see myself being moulded as a friend and a tool.

"Nick," Malcolm raised his head; he had a habit of staring into his drink. "Treacherous."

"Son of a whore," Nate said, his chin as big as a shoe.

"Nick's not so bad," I said. "If I were you, I'd watch Big Bill."

"Hey, Big Bill. That's a good one," Nate said.

"Treacherous scum."

"He takes orders from Toronto," I said. "That's where I was hired from."

"It's a shame." Wally nodded with pity and commiseration.

"What is?" I asked.

"Don't worry," Malcolm said. "People fought and died in this province against the monopolies, in the mines, in the factories. I could tell you," and he proceeded to do so. After half an hour and six more rounds, Malcolm shut one eye and proclaimed, drooling or slurring, I'm not sure which, "I'm a goddamn communist."

Big deal, I thought. "Fine," I said.

"Now, Malcolm," Nate said.

"Never mind, Nate, old Nate. Do you know about this man?" Malcolm asked me.

"No." I thought Malcolm was very drunk. He seemed much more intelligent than this.

"What do you mean by communism, boy-o?" Nate looked ready for a discussion.

"This man," Malcolm ignored his hero, "this man…" and the story of Nate emerged: Nate who'd come from a shack with eight brothers and sisters; Nate fighting fascism, first as a cook during the war, then as a member of the EBFL before it was even named. Nate's son currently did the cooking at the union centre: "The best goddamn meal you'll get in your life: roast beef, sweet and sour ribs, steaks, cake."

"What meals?" I was very interest in meals at this point. "All you have are fuckin' pickled eggs."

"At the banquets, you'll see." And back we went to Nate and a social history of Saskatchewan, concluding with, "that's what this province was."

"You weren't around then, Malcolm," Wally spoke up. "I was here during the Depression. Why, you're younger than Randy here. The dust…"

"Let the boy speak," Nate said. "This place! Smells like a beer fart. Smells like an egg and popcorn fart," and Nate let one go.

"That's nice," Wally said.

"Goddamn right."

Malcolm wasn't as drunk as he seemed. "What are you going to do about these men?" he asked.

"What do you mean what am I going to do? Come on, Malcolm. I'll be as honest as I can. The fact that I'm—"

"Sure, sure," Malcolm said.

Silence. Malcolm hunched over his beer, supposedly comatose and surly but he may have been up to something. The guy was compelling, and he had me very uncomfortable, just as he wanted. Wally murmured about there being "no such thing as objective journalism," and pushed a peanut around with a fat finger.

"You're telling me!" I said to Wally. "That's in your favour."

Nate deigned to listen to all this. Regal, his big frame at ease, he decided to show his importance.

"I know the mayor."

"Oh yeah." I didn't know the mayor, though he called me by my first name when he said hello at council meetings.

"And an alcoholic-Bible-thumping-little-asshole he is."

"I didn't know he was an alcoholic. But, come to think of it, his face is bright red."

"His tee-totalin'-asshole-undertaker-son is on council too, you know."

"I know."

"The prick."

Malcolm continued to hang his head. He was leaning further and further forward, his nose almost resting on the rim of his shot glass, and his face sagged so heavily he seemed to have jowls like a bulldog.

"You know they tried to cut my water off," Nate said.

"Oh."

"By the Christ, they soon knew better." Then he leaned toward me, his long teeth glinting mischievously. All I could think of was that his ears looked pointed; he was a satyr with his huge flat features, a satyr afflicted by giantism.

"Heh hee hee. I went down there. I'd gone in for my morning shit and, by Christ, the water was off! I went down there right away, slippers and all. Right into the office I went and I said: 'All right, let's see the mayor.'"

There followed a story in which the mayor arranged for Nate to have his water turned back on, if he made a deposit on his water bill. The city of Elk Brain learned never to mess with Big Nate Purgatoire before he'd had his shit.

"I gotta go," I said. "I'm drunk."

Nate was grinning, so pleased with himself as to seem malevolent. Malcolm rolled a sneering eye at me and went back to his coma. Wally said nothing, vague and demure in his neat shirt. He has to live with his mother, I thought.

CHAPTER FOUR

Wally didn't live with his mother, which I hoped would have explained the failures of civilization. I mean, whatever civility and intelligence he may have had wasn't exactly effective. I didn't see him or big Nate again for a while, but Malcolm made his presence felt.

He'd either ignore me when I went into the press room, or call me over and put his arm around my shoulder. This was to show me my place or make sure of my allegiance, whatever mood he was in. I'll admit the guy could be charming and friendly, offering me part of his toasted western during morning coffee breaks, inviting me to share jokes with the boys, winking whenever Big Bill went by. But the pressure was on, and I didn't exactly like being turned into a fifth column for the press room.

Life went on, as it does. One of the typesetters died, a sad old guy whose hobby was overwork. I didn't know him and wasn't invited to the funeral. None of the editorial staff was, though I think Big Bill made an appearance to hand out cigars. Council was in a slow period, the big news every year being the spring flood debates. The dry light of Elk Brain began to honey with fall; the small trees were changing, each morning frost clung in webs to the shrivelled apples that had fallen on my front lawn.

The main feature of my life was that I was magnificently un-laid. Since Larry and I drank a bit together, every chance we had, I approached him with this problem.

"Well, now you know how I miss Kitty," he said, knocking one back and reaching for a nearby ass. "I think I can set you up."

The ass continued on its way unmolested. "Yeah?" I said.

"Yeah. Kitty's coming to town and I'm getting her to bring a friend. Wow," he winked as if he'd fucked the friend.

"Have you fucked her?"

"She's a fucked-up chick."

I was prepared to love her. Her name was Laurie Crawford, and she was arriving with the mythical Kitty the coming Friday. We were all to meet at the Wagon Wheel at 11.

Kitty turned out to be much prettier than I expected, a big, very blond girl with tiny features. She had one of those large soft Estonian bodies that seem made for white and red peasant costumes. She wore a white jump suit with a red belt. Laurie was slender, younger than I'd thought, and even in the dark light of the Wagon Wheel lounge I could see she affected a lot of makeup.

After introductions the first thing Larry and I did was to show how important we were.

"Goddamn," Larry said. "I've gotta cover the game tomorrow. You girls don't mind going I hope? It should be okay, we'll have a good time. 'Course, you'll get in free."

"Damn the mayor," I said.

"Randy here's the city hall reporter," Larry helped me along.

"The old fart wants me to go out to his house tomorrow for some goddamn reception."

"Are you going to go?" Larry asked.

"Naw, I don't need to."

"Well, come to the game!"

Kitty was quiet and smiled at Larry. Laurie was making an effort to look very sophisticated. She crossed her legs and leaned back, her magenta skirt blue as plum in the shadows. I looked at her legs and noticed she had big feet. Another chick with big feet. She wore a lot of perfume.

"I'm into music," she said in response to a question.

"Larry here used to be in a band, you know," I said.

She smiled condescendingly, but a curl in her lip wasn't unfriendly. "I know. Kitty sings."

"Do you?"

"Some."

"Country and western, or Bach?" God, I was witty that night.

"A little of each."

And she really did know a lot about music. She and Kitty both.

"I can't even invert a triad, ha ha," I said, showing her I knew what a triad was.

"Let's dance, honey." Larry was pulling Kitty up. He licked his moustache and told her it hadn't been growing so well. Kitty looked demurely down but didn't seem displeased. These girls deserve better than this, I thought.

"Like to dance?" I asked Laurie, and all four of us were out on the floor, the only ones there. Of course, I tried to talk while we were dancing, an impossibility. Laurie concentrated on tossing her hair, pouting sexily, and watching her feet. Larry bounced around Kitty's slow pistoning form like a gnat. He jumped, he twitched, he performed as if he had an audience of 100,000 after his 98-pound body.

"Let's sit down," I said to Laurie. She smiled knowledgably about what I don't know. Without a word we went back to our table.

I started to talk about city council and baroque music a mile a minute. Though she tried to argue with me about the music Laurie didn't have a chance. She seemed happiest when I was quiet and she could give me her knowing smile, her thin mouth looking like a neat wound in the powdery chalk of her face.

Larry and Kitty sat down.

"Jesus Christ, Nick's here," Larry said.

"Where?"

"By the bar."

We then explained that Nick was our editor and that we called him by his first name.

"He must have Mary out for her monthly drink," I said, and added for the girls' benefit, "Mary's his wife and rumour has it Nick doesn't take her out much."

"We go out a lot," Kitty smiled at Larry and nudged him. I was about to say, 'What's the joke?' but she began to purr like a cat. I hear her mumble "Daddy," her soft blue eyes bright as stones.

"Let's get out of here," I said to Larry.

"Don't you want to have a drink with Nick?"

"No."

"Where do you want to go?" Laurie asked. "You mean this town has more than one decent bar?"

"More than Muskeg," Larry said. Kitty and Laurie were from Muskeg.

"More than Winnipeg?" Kitty joined the fray. Larry was from Winnipeg.

"Never mind," I interrupted this repartee. "Let's go down to the union centre. They've got a live band tonight."

The live band was a disaster, one of those sausage lover's specials with two polkas for a repertoire. Laurie wasn't too pleased, Laurie with all her perfume and the bony haunted look to her face. Kitty seemed to get larger and more serious. It didn't affect old Lar. He laughed, ordered drinks, talked to everyone and demonstrated a trick he thought would endear him to any union hall: how to belch at will.

We sat under the beautiful mural. It was so dark I could hardly see, the wonderful Day-Glo colours absorbing all the light. I began to talk again.

Talk at that girl I did: about Bach, about how I could anticipate Tchaikovsky's orchestration, about how *Jesu, Joy of Man's Desiring* was my favourite tune.

"Your favourite tune?"

"Sure, I'll tell you why." And I explained the circumstances of my first hearing it, involving the images of sunlight, morning, hope, and orange juice.

In the midst of all this Larry leans over. "You know she fucks like a mink."

"Right."

Larry winked. I was getting sick of his winking.

My theory of music and association stopped developing when I asked Laurie about her boyfriend, or, as she put it, the guy she lived with, off and on. It turned out he had a lot of problems, and treated her badly. Mentioning him was not a good move, but I wanted to know about Laurie and self-destructively plunged in.

She lit a cigarette and told me more than anyone could possibly want to know. Smoke curled round her thin mouth; her lips had a gloss like enamel in the black light.

"How did you meet this guy?" I asked sadly, looking round the room. I wasn't looking around simply because her story was boring, but because I knew I had effectively cut myself out of her life. Now I was a spectator for a tragic heroine. All I could do was appreciate her sufferings. I couldn't cause them.

These musings occupied me as Laurie smoked, crossed and uncrossed her legs, kept on talking. Her past was definitely shabby.

"Why don't you forget him?" I said.

"Oh God," she said. I think she was getting disgusted.

"The others weren't any better, eh?"

This shut her up, unfortunately. I wanted her to go on. Though her way of telling of her affairs had the lulling effect of a chant, I could see her in the situations she described: mornings in dingy rooms, wondering why, making herself not think about it, enjoying her walk home.

"I can understand what you're talking about," I said.

Laurie gave me the benefit of her profile, as if modeling.

The way out of this impasse stood up at another table. Big Nate Purgatoire, hitching up his pants, the monarch of all he surveyed, saw my hand twitch hesitantly in his direction. Over he came, with Malcolm in tow. Compared with these two maybe Laurie would forget the role I'd fallen into. And Brennen, who liked to be one of the regulars wherever he was, would be impressed.

"Hello, fellas!" I said. "How are ya?"

I panicked. If Larry could belch at will what would Nate do to overshadow him? I hoped we wouldn't get into party tricks.

Things weren't so bad. The worst Nate did was call Laurie "little lady." Malcolm quickly affected the comatose slouch he used when around liquor.

Then Larry started bragging about his labour affiliations. Malcolm lifted his lids a millimetre and swept in.

"Maybe you can do a little something to help us."

"Sure, yes, sure." Larry had a hand on Kitty's shoulder, holding his cigarette like a cigar, the chairman of the board. "What's that?"

"We'll let you know."

"I hear there's going to be a strike." Larry started drawing little circles with his fingertips on Kitty's back.

"We'll let you know."

"What is this?" I said. "A fucking spy novel? It looks like there's going to be a strike. Everybody knows that, Malcolm. The union hasn't had a contract for how long?"

· "We've been negotiating."

"Oh Christ!" I said.

"I guess we shoulda stayed and had a drink with Nick, eh," Larry Brennen said, still amiable, his face all creases and teeth and his little scraggly moustache.

Malcolm sneered, the first smile I have ever seen that was evil. His features were Chinese.

Larry didn't notice. Laurie and Kitty weren't as disturbed by these two as I thought they'd be, nor were they amused. My anticipation of how they'd react may have irritated them, I was jiggling my knee under the table a hundred miles and hour, but they didn't show any response. They just settled into a scene they were familiar with: not saying much in a bar, preoccupied with indifference and how they looked.

Serene creature that I am, I suggested we leave. Malcolm and Larry said goodbye to each other cordially enough, and the four of us went back to Larry's for beer.

As we drove over – thanks to me it seems we hardly stopped moving that night – I tried to get old One Lung to talk about Nick and Malcolm.

He was having one of his periodic coughing fits and smiled over at me as he clutched the wheel, hacking.

"Watch the road!" Laurie was getting impatient.

"Why didn't you go in for nursing," I said, charming her.

"You gotta stop smoking, hon." Kitty gave Larry the light he was signalling for.

"Shit," he said, once he had a cigarette. "Nick's a nice guy."

"Well, Malcolm gets to me," I said. "I always want to compete with him. He's a bully."

"Don't worry about it."

Before we could complete this intense character analysis we got to Larry's apartment. It was bleak, high ceilinged, bare. There were oak panels on the wall, but Larry quickly turned off the one lightbulb that gave them a buttery sheen. The gloom was lit only by the glare through the kitchen door.

"Beer's in the fridge," Larry said. "Anyone want a sandwich?" and he headed in to make himself one.

Kitty sat on the couch, Larry's fold-out bed, and adjusted her nylons. They were the length of knee socks. After she'd pulled them tight, she fumbled in her travelling case for little gold lamé slippers. I could see those slippers, or their equivalent, in 20 years when Kitty had gained 30 pounds: crushed at the heel, minus many spangles, soiled as old sheets.

Laurie joined Kitty on the couch, and I heard the words "woman" and "hard" arise from their conversation amid much head shaking and commiseration.

Larry emerged from the kitchen with a beer and a mayonnaise sandwich. "May-onn-aise," he said. "The best."

"Ecch," I said.

"I'll have a sandwich," said Laurie, standing up.

"Look," Lar said, leader of men that he was. "Let's all go in the kitchen and we'll make a mess of sandwiches. We can come back in here later." His statement was followed by a wink. This particular reference to the inevitable coitus was becoming singularly overfamiliar.

"Marvellous," I said, glad for a chance to stop fiddling in the dark with Larry's tape deck.

We spread the ingredients out on the kitchen table for our little party. The girls did some dishes. As Larry was spreading mayonnaise in an especially thick layer he said, with a flourish of his knife, "Hey, Laurie, like mayonnaise?"

"Ummm," and she came over, dipped her finger in the jar and licked it. "I like chocolate sauce better."

Larry and Kitty and Laurie all beamed, sharing the secret.

"What?" I was annoyed.

Larry looked at me, proud of her performance, I almost expected him to say: "See what God hath wrought."

Laurie did the finger-licking bit again.

"Okay," Larry turned to Kitty. "It's time you and I had a talk."

Kitty gave a tight little girl's smile of delight. She looked like she was going to squeak.

"We're going next door," he said to me. "My buddy's gone for the weekend. You and Laurie make yourself at home here."

"But Daddy," Kitty said, "what about my sandwich?"

"Never mind the sandwich. Let's go."

They left and, like the old smoothie I am, I said to Laurie, "Let's go sit in the living room."

She shrugged with that indifference I had such talent in bringing out. This attitude was expressed again when I kissed her. She pushed me away.

"Why?" I whispered. Of course we'd been so intimate all evening.

"Because," she said.

"It really turned me on the way you licked your finger," I said.

She shrugged.

"You look good in dark colours."

"I know."

"Let's make love."

"Uh-uh. No."

"Why not?"

"Because."

"Look, I know we're strangers, Laurie, but so what?"

"No."

"Listen. It's all right with strangers." I paused. "Listen to this:

"Lay your sleeping head, my love

Human on my faithless arm"

and I tolled Auden's poem out into the bleak room.

"Well?" I said when I had finished.

Laurie was very still.

"Are you crying?" I asked tenderly.

She was staring at her shoe.

"What are you thinking?"

"About my past."

"Tell me about it." I tried to kiss her.

She pushed me away.

"Jesus!" If I had had the poetry book with me, I'd have thrown it across the room. "Well, I better be going."

I left her sitting on the frayed couch, her long legs stretched out in front of her. Her profile was grey from the kitchen light. You could see the powder on her face, and her mouth, glossy and set.

The first thing Larry said after I told him I was hitting the road was, "Did you fuck her?" He was bare chested.

"No," I said. "Have you?"

"No," he said. "But I think I could have a couple of times. I know a lot of guys who have."

"Well, I haven't." I was feeling kinda sick, a sweetish mixture of tenderness and rage.

"Play it cool," he said. "Maybe you came on too strong."

"Maybe," I said. "But I'm going home."

"Okay, pal. See you tomorrow."

The night was fresh, with that sense of vastness and distance you get in the prairies. Looking down the street, down a slight hill, I had the illusion I was on a bluff overlooking the whole country, blue in the night. But I was in a hollow, and the wind blew far above. There was a moon, but its illumination didn't affect a wheat colour in the dark, the dry stalks of grass, boards, the small leaves of trees.

I was dizzy, the sky rushed toward me. For the first time in my life I wasn't afraid of the dark.

I walked home, quoting for awhile the poem I'd told Laurie, pulling my jacket around me against the cold and the rustling of the leaves.

Life certainly wasn't like some of the books I'd read, I thought. It was no novel. People just dropped in and out of your life and you never saw them again. I'd never see Laurie again, though I wanted to. She was going back to Muskeg on Monday, and Larry'd probably set her up with Zeke tomorrow. Give him a try. In spite of myself I was enthusiastic about her, yet at the same time I felt a marvellous indifference. I was glad to be alone.

CHAPTER FIVE

Things really began to get complicated in Elk Brain. Laurie and I started living together, and the strike loomed closer and closer. There were editorial meetings at Nick's house after hours, Mary providing the hot chocolate and cookies, and once we even went to a bar. Winter was coming.

Laurie moved into my place before the frost and before the kaffeeklatsches Nick kept providing became a way of life. The strike would threaten, recede, and I began to think it would never happen. Laurie brought with her an undecipherable past, two suitcases, a botched degree and a sullen methodology in the way she went about things. It was effective. Within two days she was employed as a waitress at the new Holiday Inn on the highway. Her salary was substantially greater than mine.

As it turned out she had gone to the game with Zeke the day after we'd met; and Zeke had fucked her. Larry, of course, informed me of Zeke's success, and I approached Zeke on this matter one day in the archives of the *Tribune*.

"How did you do it?"

Zeke looked up from a 1915 edition of the paper. He was working on a *Remember When* feature. Every day we ran a small item on what had happened on that particular day in Elk Brain 10, 15, 30, 40, 60 years ago. It was a job for junior reporters, and Zeke took it seriously.

"Don't take that crap so seriously," I said. "Tell me about Laurie."

"They had Boy Scout bottle drives even then," he said.

"Was she good in bed? Where did you do it?"

"At Larry's."

"Yeah?"

"Yeah. You know Larry isn't showing up at these meetings Nick keeps calling."

"Neither does Pounder. We don't know dick about what's going on anyway. Nobody tells us anything except that there's going to be a strike; then Tinkus digs in, Mary runs around, Barbara goes home, and Nick gets quiet."

"Yeah," Zeke said.

"Have the girls gone back to Muskeg?"

"Yeah."

"You know you're a fucking great conversationalist, Zeke. For one of my friends here, one of my only friends, you're a great conversationalist."

"So what do you want me to tell you, man?" His honest, evasive little ethnic mouth was furtive. I saw the whites of his eyes. His nose was pointed and shiny.

"Come on, Zeke. What happened?"

He spilled the beans. He shouldn't have worried, I liked him. It was man to man.

On that Sunday afternoon, after Zeke had spent two days squiring Laurie around, they were back lying on Larry's foldout. Who knows where Larry was. Laurie was talking about her boyfriend, and about sexual problems generally. Zeke had his arms around her. They hadn't really kissed, he said.

"Well, do you want to?" Laurie asked.

Zeke kissed her. She was a lousy kisser. "Yes," he said.

She lifted her skirt and took off her pantyhose and underwear while Zeke was lying there. He took off his pants. That was about it, he said. It was very quick. Zeke felt she didn't like it at all, "I mean, for a chick of her experience she certainly didn't get into it."

"Maybe she felt she owed it to you."

"I think she had to do it," he said, "but she didn't seem to enjoy it, and she told me she never came. Never. I can believe it."

I shook my head, "Tsk, tsk."

They had lain there for another hour or so, Laurie without pantyhose or pants, Zeke in his shirt and underwear. It began to get blue in the apartment, and chilly. Laurie told him about her bad family life, and how she felt excited about going with men, but not so excited while it was happening. Zeke got another hard-on and she whacked him off, wiped him off, and got up. It was getting dark.

"Well, you had better luck than I did," I told him.

"She said you were too intense."

"She was right. Come on, leave this 'Remember When' crap. I'll buy you a beer."

And that was supposed to be the last I'd hear or see of Laurie Crawford.

She was back in two weeks, with Kitty in tow. I heard about the return from Larry. We were both working late: he getting his stories off the wire, where he got most of his stories: me writing up a council meeting.

"What a surprise," I said. "Did she come to see Zeke?"

"I don't know," and he had a sip of beer. Our habit of bringing a case of 12 into the newsroom whenever we worked late was turning my copy into chicken tracks.

"They drive down in Kitty's car?"

"No. This was Laurie's idea. She borrowed a car and just sprung it on Kitty. I think they're both getting kinda tired of school."

They must have been, for they stayed the rest of the month. Either they'd forgotten about school, or decided to quit. I don't know what they did with their days, but at night all of us would go out together and drink at the Wagon Wheel, or the Ironwood if we were feeling rowdy. Zeke and I really began to look forward to it, sitting around like married couples, the girls always seeming to be in fresh or new clothes, us with jobs. I don't think Zeke saw Laurie except with Larry and Kitty and me. We began to laugh together.

But Larry, for all his talk of marrying Kitty, was getting sick of having her and Laurie around his apartment. He decided to take a couple of days off and take Kitty home to see his cancerous mother, and perhaps talk to her about "getting back to school and showing a little responsibility."

When they were away, I went to visit Laurie. At first the apartment seemed filled with nothing but twilight. Then I saw her sitting on her suitcase in the middle of the high-ceilinged room.

"Hi," I said. Only my head had appeared round the door, I hadn't bothered to knock. "Want to come for a drink with Zeke and me?"

"Oh no. I'm all right."

"I know. What's wrong?" I felt she'd been sitting there for hours.

"Nothing." She had on a travelling suit, as if she was going on a journey. Romantic fool that I am I imagined a train journey.

"Let's go for a drink!" I was animated all right, as animated as a religious fanatic talking about personality tests and happiness to passersby.

"Sure." Sigh.

"I'll call Zeke!" I said, bouncing up and down, as world weary as Pollyanna.

Laurie stood and faced me. Her long legs, big feet, narrow shoulders and the A-line skirt made her seem like some kind of fashion model in a drawing.

Zeke was not home when I phoned. We went down to work to look for him. The newsroom and the cubbyholes of the *Tribune* were empty.

"We can come back and check this out later," I said. "I'll try and phone him from the bar."

We had more than a few at the Wagon Wheel, and still no Zeke to be found. I tried his place several times, and the office, but there was no reply.

"Maybe he's gone for the weekend," Laurie said.

"I don't think so." This was becoming a strain. We had been rather formal alone, and I wanted to get out of the pub. "He might be working on something and not answering the phone. Let's go back to the paper and look. I'm going to pick up some beer anyway. We can have one." The great thing about Saskatchewan, its genius, is that you can buy beer to take out in the pubs. In Ontario, that province of small fields and crippling liquor laws, beer is served green and in glasses. There's no access to it, except at a few orgiastic government outlets, after 8 o'clock in the evening. I told this to Laurie in detail.

"I know," she said.

"Oh, yeah?"

"Zeke told us both, remember? He lived down east?"

"Oh, yeah."

The *Tribune* was empty. Zeke, who took his work seriously and often stayed after hours, couldn't be found. I didn't even see the cleaning woman shuffling in a corner. Flopping down at my desk, I leaned back in the chair. Laurie stood at the slot, the desk facing the room, and I felt avuncular. I began to talk about life in a small town, as if I was 60 and had my shirt sleeves held up with arm garters. The wisdom of life after hours. The teletype machines hummed and clicked in their closet. Laurie just stood there like a cut-out.

"Why don't you ever tell me about yourself?" I asked, still leaning back, making furtive motions of chewin' and whittlin', though there was certainly no grass to chew, and the only wood to whittle, the only non-metallic object in the place, was a pencil nub.

One of those unexpected moments in life took place: Laurie looked at me differently.

"There's nothing to tell," she said.

"There certainly is. Each of us has a past and neither one knows anything about it. We don't really know each other."

Lo and behold she didn't say anything like "Do we have to?" Nothing. She just looked at me as if I might be attractive. I opened two beers and handed her one. I don't think I'd ever felt so happy and attractive and grateful in my life.

"Wanna go over to my place when we finish these?"

The friendliness with which she dropped her shoulder in assent, like a butterfly dipping its wing to make a feint, the passively confident smile, made me want to say "Yahoo!" Instead, we sipped our beer and I told her about my father dying, the parade of "uncles," getting to university after seven years of high school, the seven years broken by intermittent glue sniffing and fornication.

"It was a progressive school," I said.

"Mine was as heartless," she said.

"Of course, I'm not desperate," I said.

Laurie didn't seem to care, that was the greatest compliment she had given me.

Her parents were both old, her sisters and brothers grown up when she was born, and her past threadbare and unhappy. She didn't fill me in, but I had a picture of a lonely girl, a family who didn't often speak, polished linoleum, quiet winter sunlight, much soup in the diet and a constant lack of money. At university, the first of her family to go, she had met her present boyfriend, the one waiting in Muskeg. Her sense of neutral desolation hadn't changed much. She loved music.

"He's a weedy little guy," she said.

"Sounds like Larry." He sounded a lot more indifferent than Larry, from the same hopeless background as herself.

As we stared at each other under the banks of light in that newsroom she was poised and expectant. Her mouth pursed at our secret, the makeup round her eyes dark and granular in the harsh light.

"Let's get going," I said. Neither of us was afraid, we both knew we could have each other.

On the way out we stopped in the vestibule. Her face felt ungiving and hard, her jaw smooth and bony as I groped for her mouth. Her lips tasted waxy, like smooth bands of muscle round her teeth. Then her tongue came forward and filled my mouth. I pressed her against the wall, feeling her long flat torso through her clothes.

"I can't believe this," I said, Laurie leaning back, head down, her thick hair bobbing forward.

We walked home with our arms around each other, springing off the balls of our feet as if we were hiking Hitler Youth heading into the Alps for a day's outing. Linked, comrades, we pushed along the midnight streets. We drank and drank and drank.

I didn't turn the lights on at my place and we stumbled around, necking, opening beer, drinking, finally falling into the bed. The curtains were wide open and the moon was full.

"Wait a minute," Laurie said as I tugged and poked at the catch in her skirt. I was dizzy and had to lie back for a moment.

We were both naked in the wash from the window, her bush thin, her navel tiny and her breasts small. Laurie's body was very soft and long and her hair was darker than the shadows, as rich and full as earth. She touched me and I've never had such a hard-on, beer or no beer. Just the two of us naked in the light of the street lamp and the moon.

Uncle Randy tried to put it in her. We were making out all right, and I liked the feel of her back, the curve where her back swept out and became her ass. But our tender love wasn't working that well.

"No, no," she said and turned over, burying her face in the pillow.

I rolled on top of her, my cock between the mounds of her ass, and pushed open her legs with my knees. "Oh darling," I murmured into the nape of her neck. Her back was beautiful, her lush soft hair, but I was beginning to think of nothing but the cleft between her legs.

I must have been bumping against her anus, I never know where anything is in the dark, because she gasped, "Oh yes." As is the way during the best sex, we were both other people yet completely ourselves.

This is my chance, I thought, and I pushed a little harder. "Ohh no," she said, meaning yes, "Oh, teach me."

"What?" I said, too fortunate to believe my ears.

"Ohh."

"Umm."

"Teach me."

Teach me! "Wait a minute." I got up to get something, Vaseline, butter, I didn't care. All I could find was a bottle of cooking oil. Bumping my way back to bed I poured a little oil on my fingertips and dabbed it on Laurie, a libation.

She lay there with her bum slightly raised, her thighs hanging gently from her beautiful bones. I put more oil on my cock, ran my tongue up her back, and lay on her.

"Relax," I said as I pushed. I had it in. She was so tight and I reached under to feel the soft, imperceptible loose of her belly. I sunk in her.

"Teach me, master."

Did I hear that? Every pathetic fantasy I've ever had, of being either on top or under at a time like this, came roaring home.

I grabbed Laurie's hips and lifted her up. I poured on most of the oil, the bedsheets were gooey with it. Her ass waved in the moonlight. Laurie rested her cheek on my pillow, lost in her own dream. That ass waved. Teach me master!

Master couldn't keep it up.

I poured on the rest, the whole fucking bottle of Mazola, I was mixing a crazy salad, but the big fella bounced off each cheek.

I couldn't even find it.

She waited, bum in the breeze. Teach me, master.

I hit both cheeks again, holding desperately to her flanks, aware of her soft inner knees, her big feet, spread on each side of my kneeling body.

"Umm," I said. "Wait a minute."

It was no good. "It's no good," I said, but she didn't seem to mind, not that she ever had.

We fell asleep in each other's arms. At what must have been 4 or 5 o'clock I awoke and saw her sitting on the edge of the bed, smoking. Laurie was hunched forward. The room was silver and grey. I touched her spine and fell asleep again, aware that the bed was sticky and clammy from the oil, that my hangover hadn't hit yet, and that when it did it would be magnificent.

CHAPTER SIX

Breakfast was a couple of 222s. Laurie got up and walked me to work, though I told her she should stay in my sodden bed. As she limped along beside me – trouble with corns or bunions or something – I asked her to stay at my place. She hadn't said much, drawn, wearing her night-time clothes in a sullen morning, but she took the key.

"Looks like rain," I said. We were holding hands. It was humid and bleak. She drew her mouth up, her forehead, cheeks clammy. We looked like nothing so much as elderly friends.

Hangover! I was so frail I made an 80-pound loss from cancer seem robust. They weren't even funny anymore, these hangovers; I was losing days, whole days, and nothing could stop the tremulous nausea, the fatigue that remained and remained. Nick asked me if I was all right, then told me to go home. He had an assignment for me in the evening. I agreed I had a touch of the flu and went back. Laurie wasn't there, she must have been at Larry's collecting her things. I was so sick I just tore off the sheets, lay on the mattress and embraced a sludgy oblivion. It was cold in that room, the colour of ashes.

When I got up to go to work again Laurie still hadn't returned. I left her a pile of sheets on the floor and a note signed love.

My assignment was, of course, a council meeting. On my way over to city hall I was waylaid by Malcolm McSweeny.

"Pssst. Come on down to the union centre."

I wanted to say, "You're ridiculous, Malcolm." But in spite of his Sicilian sibilants the guy had authority. "Why?" I asked.

"It's going to happen."

"What?"

"Come on down to the union centre. For a beer."

"Look, I have a special council meeting. I don't want any beer. I'm hungover."

"Huh! Hangover!"

"Don't you get them?"

"Yes."

"So I gotta go."

"This is important," Malcolm said.

The news, over a table full of tepid draft I was reluctant to even look at, was that there was going to be a strike.

My impatience showed. "Jesus Christ!" I almost screamed. "You think I don't know that? That's all we've been hearing from Bill and Nick for months. They're fuckin' Information Canada compared to you guys. What do you want from me?"

I grabbed a draft and downed it. Malcolm indulged me by ordering more. "You can help us," he said.

"Man, I hate that company," I said. "They aren't telling us anything and neither are you."

"There'll be a strike."

"I know, asshole. You're the one supposed to be calling it. You'll probably get locked out if you don't make up your mind soon."

"It doesn't matter. We're going out either way."

"When?"

He acted as if he knew, but he didn't answer.

"I'm leaving," I said.

"Treacherous," he said.

"What? Planning to lock you out? They probably hope it'll scare you."

"Treacherous."

"Who? Me or the Toronto Office? You know all the decisions are made there?"

"Scum."

"That's profound, Malcolm, that's very profound. I think I'm just going to start accepting that things are shitty in this life and stop wondering why they are."

"Don't cross the picket line."

"The *Tribune* in the person of one Nick Zudwicki said we didn't have to. How's that?" I wanted to call him a moron. But his stare bespoke, along with its manipulative brightness, compassion. A pitiless compassion to be sure, one that pushed you around. "Why do you always make me feel I have to stand up to you, Malcolm?"

He wasn't having any of that nonsense. If anyone was going to do the confronting it was Malcolm. He went into his boozy slump of disgust. He'd had one drink. I gulped a couple more.

"I don't intend to cross the picket line," I said. "I've thought about this, and I made up my mind long before I talked to you, Malcolm. I'm not sure I really believe Nick when he says there'll be no repercussions." At this point Malcolm looked up at me, if you can look up at a person as if he was a naïve worm. "I guess Nick figures none of us will stay out, but I don't intend to cross. I phoned a friend of mine in Toronto about this – a radical with vaginal warts, ha ha." The levity drew no response; he didn't want to hear about the warts. "I've decided not to cross, I don't know about the others." My voice quickly tried for a bass timbre.

"You'll work for us?"

"I won't cross."

"Help us."

"I'm not protected. I don't have a union, no strike pay, nothing."

"We can help you."

"How?"

"Wait."

"Look, I gotta go, Malcolm. I gotta get to this meeting."

"Have another drink."

"Okay. Then I gotta go."

The sun was setting outside. I ran down to council, suit jacket streaming behind me, pretending I was back in high school running the 880. My sweat began to feel clean; the oily residue I secrete all day when I'm hungover, as if I haven't washed, was going away. The wind was fresh, the sky pale and endless. I reminded myself that I was half drunk, and kept asking questions aloud like "Why do you have such a tender sensibility, Malcolm?" Our laconic conversations had all the reality of a TV cop show. Yet the events would be real enough.

City hall appeared deserted. I wandered in the hallways for awhile as the prairie sunset poured in, polishing the floors and coating the green walls. The corridor smelt of disinfectant, and the massive sunset blinding me with its reflection had nothing to do with these halls, nothing to do with the people who'd waited here for magistrate's court, nothing to do with the windowless, humming council chamber I went into. The seat of government smelt of ozone and cigarette smoke from the air conditioner. Half the aldermen were away.

"I miss anything?" I blurted to the radio reporter sitting in the press kennel with his equipment. Before he could answer I confided, "Been having a couple of beers down the union centre. Might be a strike." I don't know if I winked about the behaviour of journalists or the tip on the strike. He was not amused.

Needless to say I had missed nothing. My colleague ignored me as I sat there and consciously exuded fumes. When I interviewed a council member later, trying to get a story, all I could say was, "Might be a strike, eh? I mean, be a beer strike." I didn't get a story.

Nobody wanted to talk to me. My theatricality had prevented me from taking a note.

Three weeks later it all came down.

I can't say I wasn't warned. One Tuesday after lunch Nick called me into his office, something he seldom did.

"Take the afternoon off, Randy," he said, blinking.

"Thanks, Nick." I'd only worked the last five nights in a row. "Is that all?"

My editor's eyes shouldn't have been so blue, not in a face that pasty. They were like glass beads in dough, dough with large pores. A guilt more obvious than the usual furtiveness played about in his cheeks; they fluttered.

"You know we're close to a strike."

"I'll say. What's happening?"

"By the way, I think you should do that story on the fitness program at the Y. Why don't you go over there tonight." He fiddled with pencils in his shirt pocket.

"Will the strike be soon? What's going to happen? They haven't had a contract in a long time, eh?"

"It's up to you," Nick said. "Don't worry. I've talked about it with Bill. The company won't force anybody to cross the picket line. We always leave it up to the employee."

"It's our choice then."

"That's right," Nick said.

"But what happens if we don't come in, I mean even if we are classed as management?"

"There'll be no repercussions."

"Okay, Nick," I said. "That's generous."

"Sure, Randy." He got busy avoiding me again and I went out into the afternoon. It was sunny, flat western sunshine; I went home and slept.

The next three weeks passed pleasantly enough, one might even call them normal, and I enjoyed my life with Laurie. I also worked hard to make up for a certain lackadaisical quality in my journalistic performance. I did not want to get fired. Laurie and I had plans to go to Banff for Christmas. This was the first semi-normal, or at least healthy, plan I'd ever made; she was the first woman I'd ever lived with, and it would be my first Christmas away from home. Quite a victory. I was 28 years old.

Laurie hardly seemed to dent my life at all. She found her job, we slept together and enjoyed sporadic intercourse. Both of us felt we were marking time in the little one-room apartment, and we were both content, with something to look forward to. Seeing little of each other, we didn't interfere with each other. And I would often miss her. I was always glad when she came home and got into bed wearing her flannel nightgown. The gown rode up and felt almost velvet with her body heat. When we were together, we began to talk, usually when I was making my weekly pot roast or some other three-day dish. She'd sit on the bed and smoke as I quoted poetry and planned. I don't know if her tolerance for me was benign indifference, but I didn't get on her nerves, and I loved everything about her. Sometimes when I saw her naked she had me so charged with adoration I thought I'd burst. I loved the way she wiggled as she pulled up her pantyhose and I loved her deft way of doing things. She was so clean.

My drinking didn't abate, nor did my friendship with Zeke and Larry. Laurie didn't mind. I don't know what she'd have thought about the way I would stare worshipfully at her panties when she was away, but I didn't try them on. I'm sure she'd have been proud.

The morning of the strike I woke alone. Laurie had gone back to Muskeg to "get some things" and I was slightly worried she'd gotten mixed up with her old boyfriend and wouldn't return. It was a brilliant morning, cold as winter.

On my way to work I ran into Barbara Birdwell. We walked together and I jokingly told her to think of me as a "bold gay devil" whenever she looked at me. I had been reading a few ballads the night before. This passed as flirting to Birdwell, and I guess it was. She suitably smirked.

"Pregnant again?" I beamed.

"Oh, Randy!" She drove an elbow into my ribs. The sunlight was as bright as crystal. We rounded the corner to the *Tribune* and saw picketers.

"So what are we going to do?" I asked, bold gay devil that I am. She hunched like a ferret or hamster, some kind of rodent. I could feel her separate from me. "Should we run the gauntlet? I didn't know anything about this, did you?" Perhaps even suggesting we had a choice scared her because she bounded up the steps ahead of me, plump calves pumping. The strikers were lumbering toward us in snowmobile suits. Their placards read "Lockout!" These cumbersome men obviously didn't think it unusual us going in to work.

"Well, what do you think?" I stopped Birdwell. She was most anxious to get away. The direction of my sympathies must have been clear; she was remembering that I had once mentioned the strike, and its consequences, in public. I stood, waiting to be handed a leper's bell. But one did not acknowledge the disease. The women's editor of the *Tribune* was silent. Our morning mood and Randy Gogarty did not exist for her, and never had. Bantering was a treat for those who were safe. I followed her into the newsroom.

Tinkus was standing at his desk absorbed in a chocolate bar. He seldom said good morning to anyone. Barbara hung her coat at the opposite end of the rack from mine and sang a cheery "Hi!" to Nick, who was working at Larry's desk. The sports layout was the first thing Nick did in the morning, though it was supposed to be part of One Lung's job. The sports desk would have to be where I faced Nick.

I could hardly breathe as I went over and said, "Nick, you remember what you said about it being our choice? Well, in all good conscience, I feel, taking you for what you said, when we talked I…I…I'm not going to cross."

My audience of two was very attentive behind my back. I could hear Tinkus listening, his breath soft with cunning. Barbara had never been so busy adjusting a sheet in her typewriter. She was not typing.

"Okay, Randy." He held a sheet of copy poised in his fingertips. I can honestly say there was no threat in the way he answered, only accommodating surprise.

The way things happened next is hard to remember. I was still breathless and confused, and I went over to my desk to get some clippings. If I wasn't coming back to the *Tribune* I might need them. When I went by Birdwell I blew her a big smile. Her typewriter began to clatter.

Tinkus stared at me, his eyes popping. Tinkus was a mouth-breather, and with his swollen eyes and open mouth he looked vacant and harmless as a corpse.

As I fiddled at my desk my gestures felt undifferentiated and large. "See you around," I said to Tinkus, my face aching from my smile, my cheek muscles bunched as if I was yelling. Tinkus floated his head the other way. His back turned, the chocolate bar rose.

I noticed a slice of half-eaten gingerbread and a coffee on the city editor's desk. Nick's breakfast. That boy checked everything when he came in early. Mary must have packed him a good lunch. Now none of it had anything to do with me.

On the street I panicked. The men on the picket line recognized me and gave me a friendly high sign. I almost hated them. I had to have a job and began to run.

Canada Manpower was only a few blocks north. If I could get something, if I could get something became the rhythm of my stride. The office clothes tried to restrain me; the pants clung to my thighs, the suitcoat V'd and cut into my armpits. In spite of them I began to open up. My face was red, my gasping deep and powerful. I was outdoors in the late fall and running.

In two hours I had a job. At Manpower I explained to anybody who would listen about the strike. "It's only a little while, you see," but they did not want to hear. There was a position with the Prairie Farm Rehabilitation Board that would last till November, or until the snow stopped work. The job was out of town, but the pay was good, and hopefully one could get in on weekends. High with a sense of relief and adventure, I took it.

But I was scared, and I knew that my fantasies about the Prairie Farm Rehabilitation Board – working in the open, having a sense of weather, coming home to Laurie on weekends – were simply a way of denying that, no matter whose fault it was, things had fucked up. Jobs like this were fun because you didn't have to do them and they didn't last; there was always something else. This time I had lost the something else. I had arrived in Elk Brain in summer, briefly proved myself as a journalist, saved no money, made no real life, and by fall here I was chasing that dream I'd held for 10 years: sometime in the future I would be all right. It wasn't all right. There was no future and I was failing. Where was Laurie?

She was not at home. All I could do was wait for a phone call and wait for the morning. Alder Clump, Saskatchewan, was my destination and I had to be ready to go by 6 a.m.

CHAPTER SEVEN

Goddamn it, I didn't want to be out on this prairie. The foreman driving me to Alder Clump was friendly, and I encouraged him to talk about the west and the Depression. "How much do you pay for your boots?" I asked. "How much for your share in the farm?" On and on. I wanted him to talk. I'd done this before, felt so displaced I gushed all over strangers. And on new jobs I'd gushed all over the working class. But this time I wasn't worried about where I was going; I was worried about what I was leaving, and about Laurie. "Gee," "Me too," "That right?" I should have said: "Protect me."

I was light-headed with anxiety, and in spite of my enthusing would often stare out of the window, wide-eyed as a child, dumb. "Go on," I'd say. Bless him, the guy didn't think anything was wrong.

"Yes sir, young fella like you. No one in town, eh? You should come out to the house some Sunday."

"I'm not young," I said. "And you mentioned having daughters?"

"Yes sir, we have a real big meal. They bring their fellas and we get together. It's real good."

"Oh. Their fellas."

We'd stopped at the house before setting off and I'd met his wife. She showed me her sculptures. You put marbles in the oven till they cracked and then glued them together to make turtles. We had coffee. I made sure they knew all about my predicament at the *Tribune*. They liked me anyway. The morning was beautiful, and I mentioned it. Day after day had been beautiful. I mentioned it again.

"Gorgeous day."

"Ha ha, not always." The foreman was wrinkled and brick-faced, a feature of arid climates I do not find attractive. They all grinned like satyrs out here whenever they tried to look homey.

The landscape was dazzling, chalk white.

"That's salt," he said.

"No trees."

"No trees."

"No clumps of trees to hide in," I said. "No shade."

"Nope."

There had been nowhere to hide last night. The apartment felt like it had been stripped bare, as if I was moving out. Laurie and I had never inhabited the place. I sat on the bed, bored, and stared at the cold stove. I didn't draw the curtains or turn on a light. The stove reminded me of Laurie and all our meals, all the cups of tea I'd had by myself when I was happy.

Indulging in food is a way out of despair, so I decided to go downtown to Wong's or the Polynesian Village for an overpriced meal. Then I'd go somewhere else for dessert. As I left the apartment, I gave it one last look. The room was empty, waiting for someone else.

Elk Brain is a small city and I'd hoped to run into someone. I couldn't find Zeke or Larry at home, and I didn't want to go near the paper. For once in my life I didn't feel like drinking.

I ran into Mary Zudwicki. She looked at me with narrowed eyes, cautiously. They were all cautious bastards in this town. Her discomposure was brave, maybe she felt I wouldn't be around long. She smiled, if not timidly, at least deferentially; indulging an eccentric.

"How are you, Mary?" I went right up to her. "I guess you've heard about the strike."

"I'm going up to the high school for the night course," she said. She must have been related to Birdwell: with their similar avoidance look the two of them had to come from the same gene pool.

"Are you related to Barbara?" I asked.

"What?" Now she knew I was crazy.

"You're looking at me just like she did when I asked her about the strike."

"I'm going up to the high school for my night class," Mary said.

"The high school, eh? I've covered meetings there. It's gloomy in the auditorium."

"I'm taking dance." Mary had on this cozy fall sweater and the collar of her blouse was crisp and fresh. She looked as if she should have been out identifying with her four-year-old daughter on Halloween, munching apples. But there was a nice middle-aged look of fatigue under her eyes. All the fine-featured women I know can look brittle, especially if their hair is stiff and combed up like Mary's.

"Heard about the strike?" I was bullying this confused weak woman, bullying her. I remembered Birdwell confiding to me that, "Nick doesn't take Mary out enough."

"Mmmm." The little girl's face hardened, though she bit her lips nervously.

"What do you think about it?" I asked.

"Has Nick phoned you?" she said.

"Nick. Why would he phone me? I hope the damn thing is over soon."

"Then he hasn't gotten hold of you."

"No. Why? The main thing about this strike from the beginning has been its mystery. I'm sick of it." I smiled at her challengingly, like a salesman. All my teeth showed.

"Oh well, I though he'd got hold of you."

"What for?"

"Maybe you better call him."

"I will."

The rest of my night had been solitary.

I would call Nick when I got back to town, I thought as the truck whizzed along the highway. He probably wants me to go back to work. I think I'll go. It'll be a relief. I don't want to stay out here.

Glare shimmered off the asphalt. We were rocking and rolling.

"Mind if I open the window?" I asked the foreman. No, he didn't mind. The noise in the truck got worse.

Every mile we went west was a first for me. It was quite a thrill. "This is the farthest I've ever been in Canada," I told my companion. He seemed quite pleased.

We crossed and recrossed the CPR tracks, and for a while kept pace with four huge diesels. Another thrill.

"That's where Poundmaker tried to stop the railroad," and the foreman pointed to a stretch of track. "They just picked the bastard up, carried him to the side, and kept on going. Trouble." He shook his head sadly.

It must have been pathetic. The tall grasses grew in the cinders, their waxy stems bending to the wind. The rails gleamed.

Alder Clump was also a place of historic interest I was informed. Located in the Cypress Hills, Alder Clump was one of the first outposts of the North-West Mounted Police.

To get to it we passed through land. Our journey was the scenery. The prairie swept up in waves, bore down on us. The slopes were purple and gold.

We stopped in a town for coffee and the day seemed to stretch ahead forever. Mennonites walked the streets, celebrating in their drab clothes the undifferentiating sun, a lifetime of it. For all its sharp edges the town was quiet. The dust was less vivid here, the solid colours of the landscape had been broken.

Our trip also involved calling in on Prairie Farm Rehabilitation Board employees. These were fieldworkers and they lived in trailers. They took care of the community pastures, mending fences, ploughing firebreaks, and invariably had gone for the day when we arrived. Their wives gave us coffee. The women handed us the drinks in the cab of the truck, brushed hair out of their eyes with bluish, swollen forearms, and received the papers for their husbands. The wind blew unrelentingly.

We reached our destination in late afternoon. There had been a cattle auction in Alder Clump and it was just breaking up. We got caught in traffic momentarily near the pens. The dust raised from the trucks, the smell of straw and wet manure and fear lingering from the cattle made me feel this a shabby place. I didn't have time to confirm my opinion. We went directly to the job site.

The job was to dig a culvert. I made a good impression, though I didn't find out about it until later, by pitching right in. My superiors, the foreman and Cuzyk, the gang leader, chatted while I grabbed a shovel and climbed down the hole. The mud was cold and raw. For about an hour I pushed some dirt around and watched my fellow labourers risk being crushed by squeezing between the metal culvert and the side of the ditch. The backhoe holding the pipe seemed inadequate for the weight it was lifting. The foreman and Cuzyk continued to talk. I decided to take a leak. Why didn't they quit work?

Out of the ditch I was colder. The wind was sullen and very high up; the sky had darkened. I pissed on some grass at the edge of the prairie and looked at the site of the old Mountie fort, just a bump on the shoulder of a hill. I didn't want to stay here and decided to go back.

Our living quarters convinced me. When we finally stopped work and got back to camp, I saw that I'd have to share a trailer with three other members of the gang. I don't know what else I expected. There was a voluble Portuguese and a half-retarded, hump-shouldered father of three that the voluble Portuguese tormented. The third member of the party was a 55-year-old cowboy, the backhoe operator. He was a native of Alder Clump but, as the foreman whispered to me on the drive home, he had a drinking problem and didn't live with his family. This romantic figure, dapper and self-possessed as a jockey, complete with liver spots and the usual wizened face, asked me where I intended to make my "nest." He was referring to the three blankets we had been issued and my reluctance to handle them. I liked these guys, I thought. I really had to get away. I knew them too well already.

Instead of making my "nest" I ran into town. Past an empty lot going wild, past a little bungalow so well kept it was sad, past the deserted theatre, down the main street and into the hotel.

"Four Bo," I ordered. Bo is the Saskatchewan diminutive for a beer of supposed Slavic derivation and essence.

I'd have to make up some excuse for the foreman, and the gang leader. I'd have to go back and get my things. I'd have to find out what time the bus or train left. I'd have to call Elk Brain – I'd really messed up.

There was no need to go back and face Cuzyk. As I was thinking up ways not to accuse myself of quitting, he came into the hotel.

I needn't have worried. After stressing my situation I told him I had just received a call and had my job back.

"It's important I leave tonight," I said. "That job is my career."

He understood perfectly, dismissing all excuses with a flaccid wave of his hand. The man was pleased I included him in my plans. I was glad he had taken me seriously. We were both of us grateful.

After my explanations Cuzyk confided in me, as an educated man: his youngest daughter was having a great deal of trouble at school; things were too easy on people with unemployment insurance; he was glad I hadn't just stood around with the shovel this afternoon; people didn't want to work nowadays.

This last remark flattered me.

"How old do you think I am?" he asked.

"I dunno. Fifty something."

"I'm 62." He gave an impish grin, a frail, wiry man of 62.

"You don't look 62," I said.

"I'll drive you to the bus," he said.

"Is there a train leaving tonight?"

"No. You've missed it. There's a bus at midnight but you have to drive 12 miles up to the Trans-Canada to catch it."

"Thanks very much," I said. "But what about your sleep?"

"I don't sleep much anymore."

"Another drink?"

"I don't drink much anymore."

"Isn't it kinda hard," I asked, "a man of your age still on the road? I mean the other foreman sleeps in the hotel. You're still out at camp in a trailer."

"Naw," he winked, and I saw he didn't have much respect for the foreman. "Anyway there's nothing much to do at home."

I could believe it. Sundays at this guy's house must have been deadly. He loved to work, to pile the materials at the yard the way he wanted them, to push people longer than their break, to go without sleep. I hoped there'd be enough for him to do when he retired. There wouldn't be.

"I'll see you out at camp around 11 then," I said.

"Sure." As he left Cuzyk cocked his head around the room, making sure no other members of the crew were destroying themselves with alcohol. As he told me – too much to drink at night and you're "no damn good" the next day.

"More beer," I screamed at the waitress. She was not impressed. I tried to engage her in conversation.

"I see you can mouth all the words to all the country songs. You must know them."

"That's right."

"I'm not being facetious, but you're the first person I've met under 40 since I arrived in town."

"That so." Scooping up the Bo bottles and pirouetting away.

"Don't leave." I touched her denimed ass. She was a golden girl, built like a physical education major, in gingham and pigtails. "I know the words to country songs. Really, I do."

She looked at me with contempt.

"Is this your home?"

She left.

The bar was beginning to fill up. Now all I had to do was tell the man who'd driven me to Alder Clump that I was leaving.

The other clientele in the lounge did not please me. They were all rather large, male, exuberant, with dried cow shit stiffening their coveralls. Two of them were drooling. Worst of all they *knew* each other. I knew no one, but sensed hostility to my pale complexion, grinning vulnerability, and desire to please. At least I had mud on my coat. I left the waitress a big tip.

Before breaking the sad news to the foreman about terminating my employment I decided to try and call Laurie in Elk Brain.

No answer.

Oh well, I'd try Zeke. No answer. Larry. Nothing. Hitching up my pants I went to search out the senior representative of the Prairie Farm Rehabilitation Board in Alder Clump.

He did not answer my knock on his door. I banged harder and heard a groan from the interior.

"Hello," I said, trying the door handle. "Hello."

I heard a moan and pushed the door open slightly. "Hello."

There was no reply. All I could see was the glow of a lamp on the far dresser.

"Are you there?" I opened the door wider.

"Unh."

"Are you asleep?" The light from the corridor allowed me to make out the night table. On it were an old-fashioned shaving mug, a glass of water and a package of Bromo.

"Are you all right?" The room smelt sour. Stepping into it I could see sheets piled on the bed haphazardly. I couldn't make out a body.

"I won't be a minute," I said. "It's just that I have to go back to Elk Brain tonight. For my job on the paper." I stepped back into the hall.

"Colostomy."

"What!"

The word emerged from the piled linen of the bed. "Colostomy."

"I have to go back to Elk Brain tonight if it's all right."

"Ten years of ulcerative colitis. I've got to have a colostomy."

"I have to go back to Elk Brain tonight." All I could do was look at the light from the lamp, yellow as corn oil.

"Colostomy."

"So you've said."

There was a pause. "I'm going back. Okay?"

"Yeah."

"Thank your wife for me will you?" and I shut the door.

It was 10 o'clock. The man must have been in bed for hours, shut in that close room with his insomnia and his old man's smell and dazed terror. I hoped he understood I was leaving.

There wasn't much to do now. I decided to get a breath of air, have a couple more beer though I knew they'd make me sick on the bus, then go and collect my things.

The night was blowing like a hurricane. No stars were visible, even distant house lights seemed to flicker from the force of wind. All activity was centered at the hotel.

I went back in. The hotel had two entrances and, instead of going in the bar door as I had before, I went through the lobby.

The room I entered surprised me. It was full of Indians, about 20 of them, watching TV. There were trophies on the walls: buffalo heads, elk, mounted fish, and the panelling looked like it had come from an old caboose. At first, I thought maybe this was a recreation annex for the Indians because they were not allowed in the bar. I was wrong. These handsome people, Blackfoot from what I understood, were totally unlike the acne-ridden wrecks who'd asked me for dimes in Regina.

I had to phone Laurie and tell her what a colourful place I was in. I had to tell her that I missed her and was coming home. Again there was no answer. Zeke and Larry were out as well.

So that was that. Another misplaced adventure of Randy Gogarty's was drawing to a close and there was no one to tell it to. Of course I'm not full of self-pity. I went out to camp to collect my belongings.

Cuzyk was in his trailer when I got there, filling out forms. The nook he'd partitioned off for himself smelt of oil from the heater and machine oil and earth from his clothes. I signed a couple of papers, we threw my suitcase into the back of the truck, and we were off.

The headlights of the truck and their perimeters were all I could see in the world. My chauffeur seemed to know where he was going, and I felt us undulating over rises in the land as we made our way to the pool of fluorescence on the Trans-Canada, the filling station and bus stop, that marked our destination. We didn't talk much, and I felt very safe in the truck, moving through the darkness.

We reached my embarkation point and the gang leader decided to accompany me as I purchased a ticket and had a slice of pie. He suggested a meal. Since I was hungry from the beer I acquiesced. Cuzyk stood me to a fried chicken plate.

"You haven't touched your food," I said trying to separate my fingers from a plastic container of honey.

"Don't eat much anymore."

"So tell me about your daughter and her problems. She's in public school you said?"

"It's a shame," he said.

"How so?" I asked. Then before he had a chance to answer, "Is the man who drove me to Alder Clump really ill? When I went to his room to tell him I was going back he seemed quite distressed."

Cuzyk shook his head.

"Does that indicate something is inappropriate?" I asked him, referring to the shake of his head. "Tell me about it."

"It's sad."

"What is? That he's sick."

Again he shook his head in disapproval and pity.

"I take it you're implying the PFRB is corrupt in employing a man like that," I said.

"It's too bad," he said.

"How bad is he?"

"I don't know about sick," the job boss said.

"Well, can't he do his job?"

"What job?" The man's major contribution to our conversation continued to be a cluck and shake of the head.

"Does that question imply inefficiency?" I asked.

He smiled sagely and tugged at an earlobe; the corners of his mouth were so pointed with wisdom that he looked like a devil. "Be sure to drop by the house in Elk Brain."

"I really do appreciate the ride," I said. "Thanks a lot." I did not want to share his boredom in Elk Brain.

My wait was uneventful. I met a French Canadian with a handlebar moustache dressed totally in leather who was travelling across the country by motorcycle – at night. I asked him if he had a girlfriend because the subject reminded me of Laurie, and I enjoyed thinking about her. A woman talked to me who was waiting for her husband to come and pick her up. She'd been waiting for hours but didn't mind because her husband was "all crippled up" with arthritis and found it difficult to drive. This wrinkled woman loved the prairies, the still daylight, the quiet. "Now, what with TV, we have everything everybody else has.

When my bus arrived it was full, and I had to stand in the aisle if I didn't want to wait until the next one at 4 a.m. I stood for two hours, breathing in a considerable volume of middle-aged breath. I don't know how the sleepers below me withstood the rigors of this means of travel, but then they had no choice. We suffered innumerable delays. One wait near Elk Brain lasted an hour while the driver stood outside and talked. It was not a rest break; there was no explanation; I was furious. As the windows lightened, the passengers began to stir, waking and looking mutely at the horizon. My face was oily, my mouth tasted bad. I was glad to be home.

The streets and buildings of Elk Brain, empty and waiting for another day of commerce, were very familiar. I felt I'd been away a long time, and that they'd never mean the same to me.

CHAPTER EIGHT

"Where have you been?" I asked Laurie. She had let herself into my apartment and stood at the door. I was just coming to after my long sleep and felt like I was still on the bus. "What time is it?"

"It's 4 o'clock in the afternoon." Laurie was dressed in her magenta suit. She looked like she'd just come in from a day at the office, except there was something cold, garish, of the night in the amount of makeup she wore. The powder made the gloss on her mouth seem blue, disapproving.

"Where have you been? Oh, I feel lousy."

"I could ask you the same thing." She was very formal and stared at the key in her hand as if it was a car key and she was anxious to be leaving.

"I got in this morning from Alder Clump," I said. "Didn't you get my note? Where have you been so long?"

"So that's where you were. I got back yesterday and saw your note," Laurie started explaining carefully, like a little girl. The reserve left her body as she enunciated. "I phoned Larry. He guessed you'd gone to Manpower and we phoned up. They had your name, and two places that had hired for the PFRB. Alder Clump and Tooley. We took off to find you and stayed overnight. We went to Tooley. It's closer."

"You and Larry went to Tooley and stayed overnight?"

"Larry and I and Zeke and Kitty."

"What's Kitty doing back in town?"

"I brought her with me," Laurie said.

"You mean she came back from Muskeg with you, and you took her with you and Larry and Zeke on the trip to find me?"

"That's right. We used Zeke's car. The Tooley Caper."

"The Tooley Caper! Let's have coffee." God, did I feel unattractive. I wanted to wash.

"We just got back." She was animated and breathless. "It was great." Laurie looked as if she might have recently woken up, put her makeup on after a late dissipated night. "You weren't gone long," she said.

"I couldn't hack it. I don't need jobs like that anymore. What the Christ did you do in Tooley?"

"Drank, smoked dope, popped pills. I couldn't believe us. Bouncing along in Zeke's car. We asked after you everywhere. They thought we were crazy."

"Wonderful," I said with as much sarcasm as I could muster. Then in a fit of tenderness I went over to embrace her. She stiffened. "Why don't you take off your clothes?"

"No."

Her belt buckle bit into my soft stomach, her wool dress irritated my skin.

"Ah, come on. Take off this dress." I wanted her in her slip, I wanted to feel her bare shoulders and the silk smooth over her bum. I wanted all the wonderful little smells her clothes and body gave off as she undressed.

"Not now, Randy. I'm kinda wiped out."

"Okay," I said, hurt of course, aware of my sagging underwear, my body slack from sleep. She loosened my grip gently but her mood was not a good one. I went over to the sink to wash.

"How was Muskeg?" I asked, making myself think that I was really glad they'd looked for me. I had friends.

"All right."

"Any trouble?"

"No. Why should there be?"

"Did the old boyfriend say anything when you went to get your things?"

"Not really."

"So what happened?" I asked.

"He wants me back."

"Now, Laurie," I said carefully, "don't scare me like that. I don't need it. I'm scared enough as it is thinking of how he treated you."

"It wasn't completely like you think, Randy." She had a disinterested look about her now, even though she used my name. Laurie turned her head and looked away, as she had the night we met. I felt that if I raved she'd defend her old boyfriend, her old way of life, against the glib stranger. She wouldn't say much, but she would perversely believe in it.

"Everything went all right then."

"He wants me to have his child."

"He wants you to have his child," I mimicked her. "That's a bombshell! The pathetic abusing little rat wants you to 'have his child.' What kind of cliché is the guy? So, do you want to 'have his child'?"

"No, come on."

"Ah, reassurance. But he still has something for you, yes?"

"Yes."

"So what happened?"

"He, he sorta raped me."

"What'da ya mean 'sorta?'"

"He made me make love to him before he'd let me leave."

I could see it, her legs up over his back, Laurie indifferent but accepting, and implying in that acceptance her enjoyment. The shiny hollows of her knees.

"And you did," I said with sorrow. "You didn't have to, you know, you never have to unless you want to, or he has a knife at your throat. Are you going back to him?"

"No."

"I'm not going to freak out about this, Laurie. I feel like it but I'm not going to. I won't be able to put it out of my mind but I'm going to try to. Are you going to stay here?"

"Yes."

"You're sure you're not going back to him?"

"Yes."

"Is the reason you stay with me is because you don't have to fuck me? You can say no. I mean you don't have to fuck me now even if I want to."

"Partly, I guess."

"Well, I'm insecure. I do turn you on, right?"

"Sometimes."

"Let's forget about the whole thing, okay? I know your relationship was sick but you're with me now, let's just forget it. I don't even want to think about it. Why'd you do it?"

"It doesn't matter."

"Okay, okay. I was worried something like this would happen when you went back, and that you'd stay in Muskeg. It happened. I was right. But you're here. You're back. It really didn't matter with him, right? You're here."

"Yes!"

"Okay, okay. Let's forget it. Why'd you have to tell me?"

"You're boring," Laurie said. "If you keep going on you're going to really turn me off."

"Boring! You tell me a story like that and what'm I supposed to do."

"It didn't mean anything."

"Okay. I find that hard to believe, but okay. He wants you to have his child."

Laurie shrugged fatally, indifferently.

"He still has something for you. A guy who can say something like that still has something for you."

"In a way, but it doesn't mean anything."

"It's not even the idea that gets me, but the way he used it."

"Don't go on," she said.

"Do you know what he said *means*. What a stupid, pathetic…"

"Shut up, will you. Shut up."

"Okay. Look, okay. It doesn't matter and we can figure it out. Never mind. I'll just get my job together and we can go on. I've made my little gesture and now I can go back to work. The union never offered me any help anyway."

"You've been fired."

"What!"

"That's what Larry wanted to tell you. Nick said he 'had to let you go' and Larry wanted to tell you."

"The bastards, the fuckin' bastards. Nick and his 'no repercussions.'"

"There's a meeting tonight at Larry's house about it. The union has an organizer here and they're going to try to get the newsroom to join."

"How can we? We're not printers. And can you see Birdwell joining the union? I suppose they'll include Tinkus as well."

"Not everybody has to agree to join to get certification as a union. They'll explain it tonight. At Larry's."

"I'm fucked, I'm fucked. What are we going to do now?"

"Go to the meeting. They're really worried about you."

"I feel lousy. Let's lay down and forget about the whole mess. I don't want to think about anything."

Laurie took off her shoes and we lay down side by side.

"So tell me about the trip," I said.

"We got drunk and we had to stay in this really grotty motel."

"Did you sleep with Zeke and Larry because you had to?"

"Yes." Laurie had her back to me, and her voice was muffled by the pillow.

"Baby," I said slowly, "I think I believe you."

"We were all drunk." She turned and faced me, the makeup coarse on her face, her mouth askew where it was pushed up by the pillow. Her brown eyes glittered in her twisted face.

"What are you trying to do, Laurie?"

"Nothing. You asked."

"Have you fooled around like this before?"

"Unh huh. In Muskeg."

"With Larry and Kitty?"

"With Kitty. We were drunk."

"Who instigated it, you?"

"We were very drunk."

"Did you screw Zeke this time out?"

"No. Larry. It didn't mean anything."

"The wife-swapping little bastard. And there I am sitting on a bus. Are you in love with Larry?"

"Get serious. We were ripped. So what?"

"So what, yeah so what. 'It didn't mean anything.'" I was very tired. "I'm not a martyr, Laurie; I'm fucking St. John of the Cross, because I really don't care about this. But how could you with that fucking weasel? Now I'll have to listen to his goddamn bragging. That's what bugs me."

"Ask him about Zeke and Kitty then."

I felt I didn't want to touch Laurie. She turned and stuck her rump against me. I put my arm over her and we were quickly asleep.

When I awoke the room was dark, but I could see Laurie's clothed body in the light from the street.

I felt headachy, and indifferent to all that had gone before, and I pressed against her. She seemed asleep but rolled over on her stomach and moved her arms up to hug the pillow.

Raising her skirt up to her waist I felt for the elastic of her panty-hose. Laurie lifted herself up a bit to help me as I pulled them down. Her legs were white and smooth, and I could feel bristle on her calves. I eased my underwear down and lay on her. She clutched the pillow as if she were still asleep while my knees pressed between her legs and opened them slightly.

Reaching down I rubbed the knob of my cock against her, up and down, beginning to fit it in. Her labia were dry and soft and warm and slowly parted. I eased her legs a bit wider. She sighed and I gently began to push my knob inside her, just the tip, stretching her. She was moist inside and I could feel the folds of skin, parting, clinging to me. Slowly I moved my cock back and forth in her, just the knob. Her breathing became heavier. I eased the complete shaft into her and she lifted silently to meet me. I could imagine the shaft glistening when I pulled it out and she began to smell. She smelled sour and green and damp, and she spread her legs wider. I could feel her buttocks round and soft and it feeling almost flat between her legs, following me, stretching, opening like the petals of a flower.

➳⍫⳪

Laurie and I sat on the floor at Larry's apartment, very much a couple. As usual we were drinking beer, and as usual the light was bad. The hardwood floor seemed grey. Zeke, Kitty and Larry were on the couch, sharing it with the *Tribune*'s staff photographer, a pimply youth of 18 name Quixley.

We were restless, with the feeling we'd had a bit too much of each other. Zeke and Larry and Kitty were obviously tired and still hungover from their party, and though I hadn't participated I may as well have. Laurie pouted beside me. I wasn't sure if her resentment was toward the wait, with nothing to look forward to but the tedium of a meeting, because she couldn't chatter with Kitty, or because there'd be no entertainment later. This was not nightlife, and we'd have nothing to do but go home. We were all of us bored.

"Really, man, I'm glad you came back," Larry said to me. "We had a hell of a time looking for you. What'd you run off like that for?"

"Panic, I guess," I said. "Fucking up another job. So you enjoyed the 'Tooley Caper.'"

"Yeah!" He winked at me, baggy-eyed little dissipator. How could you stay mad at a guy when he included you in orgies at which you hadn't been present?

"Where are those assholes?" Zeke asked, his face whey pale, his pointy nose glistening.

"They're certainly late," Kitty said.

In answer there was a perfunctory knock on the door and Malcolm McSweeney, Nate Purgatoire and, I presume, the organizer, made their appearance. Quixley shivered visibly and picked at his skin.

"You're just in time, Tinker Bell," Larry said to Malcolm. "We were wondering where you were."

Malcolm ignored him, slouching into the room bow-legged, like a cowboy, with one hand in his dungarees and his arm round a case of beer.

"This is Carl," Malcolm introduced the newcomer. "He's from the International Brotherhood of Printers and Typographers." Malcolm swayed a little, conveying his now familiar aura of holding something in reserve.

"So, what's your ace in the hole?" Larry flashed out. "You look like you got something to tell us."

"Carl will explain." Malcolm went to the kitchen to open beers.

Nate greeted us all with a nod and slipped down beside Laurie on the floor, easing onto his hams and giving her an extra shake of the head. His quiet salutation was: "Goddamn."

Evidently this was to be Carl's show. His toupée was obvious, an auburn to black napkin perched on top of his skull. He wore checkered pants, a body shirt over his round compact trunk, and had a crescent-shaped scar under his right eye. I immediately associated the disfigurement with a duelling scar.

Smiling, tapping a cigarillo ash on the floor, Carl quickly memorized our names. He ignored the girls when he found they were not involved.

"It is very simple," Carl said. "All we have to do is get 90 per cent of the newsroom staff to sign the papers I've brought with me and we can apply for certification as a union. Then you'll be members of the IBPT, with full rights. You can strike with us. We'd really close the place down."

"How long does it take to get certified?" Zeke asked.

"About two weeks. We'll deliver the message to Nick and Pounder by registered letter. It'll really sock it to 'em."

"But if they find out we've joined we'll all get fired," Quixley protested.

"They won't find out," Carl said. The hint of a whisper entered his voice, as if he was mesmerizing and threatening a child. "It won't go beyond this room, will it? If we get these papers signed tonight, they can't fire you. The application would be official. And no one will find out. This Birdwell won't know; she doesn't know about our meeting. You see, once you've joined you get full protection. We'll negotiate a contract for you."

"Yeah, but what about in the meantime?" Quixley continued.

"Just go on doing your job as before," Carl answered. "Zey won't find out!" the slight accent asserted itself. "And if they do, they can't fire all the staff for applying to join a union. It's against the law."

"Yes, but..." Quixley had burst one whitehead and was working on another.

"How many hours a week do you work?" Carl asked.

"I dunno. About 65 I guess."

"How much do you make?"

"One hundred and ten clear."

"You want to keep zat up? You're exploited." Carl was calm. "Now let me explain..."

And explain he did, very sanely, very legalistically. I trusted, not so much him, but his grasp of the situation. We weren't helpless: we could fight back.

The room was quiet through all this, with Malcolm replenishing beers, Carl's voice see-sawing logically on, and the occasional diminutive "goddamn" from Nate. The big fella's bowels were rumbling, and he may have been leaking what he called "silent but deadlies" into the room as he squatted beside Laurie. But they were not deadly, perhaps out of deference to the "lady." If anything the room smelt of fatigue, the indoor sweat and airlessness that can have you reeling and thinking skittishly. Carl kept on. Zeke was the only one to interrupt.

"What about the Newspaper Guild?" he asked. "Can they help us, or Randy?"

"They're affiliated with us," Carl said. "We've contacted them and they agree it would be better for you to join our union in this case, since we're involved in the strike. We're working on closer ties and perhaps in the future these will involve you becoming members of the Guild."

"It'd be nice to get into the Guild," Zeke said wistfully, and I remembered the poor guy telling me how he'd dropped out of journalism at Western.

More explanations followed. Finally I said, "All right. I've had enough of meetings. I'm going to sign my application. It's clear enough." Hopefully the room would break up into conversation at this point; I was beginning to get drunk and wanted at least the semblance of a party.

"We have to do this properly," Carl said. "You have to sign privately, after I've explained to you what it is – like a polling booth. We could use the kitchen."

"Let's go," I said getting up stiffly. "Christ I've been sitting too long."

No one said a word and Carl followed me in. I told him I knew what was involved, and he put the very official looking form on the kitchen table, pushing the mayonnaise and butter out of the way.

"I know what this means," I confided, "and if we can get the others to sign we do have a chance, don't we?"

"Yes. And we can get you reinstated."

"Well, I want to fight those pricks. Say, don't you drink, Carl?"

"Yes, a little. I can do without it."

"How can you stand all the meetings you must sit through without a drink?"

"It doesn't interest me."

"Meetings leave me cold too. You know I was city hall reporter?"

"I mean ze liquor doesn't interest me."

"Yeah? How do you like your job, Carl? I mean the meetings."

"Ever since I come to Canada, I've had a convertible."

"You've always had a job, huh?"

"Zat's correct." The guy's accent would ebb and flow, coming on strong when he was questioned, unlike the sweet reason and smooth English of his monologues. His pot-bellied smug little frame seemed to stand very formally in front of me.

"Oh well," I smiled at him falsely, aggressively. "It's a good thing to join the union, to protect ourselves. Give me the paper."

I signed and we went back into the living room. The others were still sitting around as if they were paralyzed.

"Come on," I said. "I know I've committed myself by not crossing the picket line, and I've already lost my job. But you guys can only be protected. Just keep quiet and keep working. It won't go beyond this room and then Nick and Pounder will receive the news. They won't know what hit them."

"I'd like to see their faces," Laurie said.

Nate shifted his haunches toward her in approval. "Goddamn."

"I'll sign," Zeke said. "They're a bunch of bastards anyway." Zeke had not been getting the assignments he wanted.

"Thanks, Zeke," I said. "What about you, Quixley?"

"Sure, uh, okay," he said. "I guess so. No one'll find out, eh?"

"No," I said.

"No," Carl said.

"No," Malcolm said.

The three of us made a perfect chorus of ding dong bell the way we chimed in, though I thought Malcolm looked a bit peeved that he hadn't added to the assuring harmony before Carl.

Zeke went into the kitchen with Carl while Quixley sat and fiddled with his face, examining his fingertips after he'd felt the skin to see what oil or matter adhered. Larry sat back in the sofa, making every effort to look sour and jowly. I recognized it as Larry's version of a hard-headed businessman, but it's pretty hard to look jowly when your face is practically fleshless. I didn't know what was going through his mind. Nate digested away and every few seconds shook his head in agreement with himself and his innards, a quick approving "Yep." Laurie was not interested, but Nate edged closer, sure at least that she wanted to talk to him.

"So, Malcolm," I went over to him, "what'da ya think?"

The young Turk got up and gave me the usual knowing look. Everybody knew things out here; nobody could talk. He tugged at his dungarees, I almost expected a "goddamn."

"How come he's running things, Malcolm?"

"Don't worry about it."

"It's good you brought this guy in; he really knows his stuff. Why did you?"

"That's all right."

"Couldn't you have done it, Malcolm?"

"He wants to run the whole show."

"Is he good at it, Malcolm?"

"They parachute these guys in, but we do the slugging. He's involved in a strike here, one in B.C. He's based in Edmonton. But we're here all the time."

"He seems to know what he's doing."

"Yeah." Malcolm again tugged at his dungarees. "This is our strike, the men who walk the line."

"I'm sure Carl knows that."

"Don't worry about it."

"Look, man. I've put out for you in this strike. What are you so surly about?"

"Nothing. Carl's a bit of a hotshot, that's all." Then Malcolm tried to be friendly, putting his hand on my shoulder before sitting.

"I'll get us some beer," I said.

While Malcolm and I had been talking Quixley and Zeke had signed their applications. Malcolm was busy with his comatose act, waiting for the appropriate moment to raise his shaggy head and lash out.

"Beer, Zeke?" I asked, twitching my head in imitation of Nate's "goddamn." The trouble is that's how I felt, "goddamn."

"Sure."

"Quixley, my boy?"

"Uh, sure, uh, okay." His chin was bleeding.

"Where's Carl?"

"He's gone to the toilet," Quixley said.

"To get rid of some of that hot air I hope." Larry turned away in disgust, facing Kitty on the sofa. "Got a light?"

"What's the matter with you?" I asked. "What he says is clear enough. Aren't you going to apply with us?"

"I have a few more questions, that's all." Larry held his cigarette as if it was a cigar and, although it was barely burning, he flicked it to deposit the ash on the floor. It was hard to tell if this was a parody of Carl, or simply Larry taking himself seriously. But speak of the devil, Carl rejoined us.

"So," he said, clapping his hands together. "You're next." He smiled at Larry. His toupée was askew, and he smelt of soap and the close atmosphere of the washroom. He'd obviously washed his hands, they were plump and gleaming, and tucked in his shirt.

"Just a minute, people, just a goddamn minute. I have a few little questions I'd like to clear up."

Kitty sat demurely; her bulk gathered close to her man.

"It's very zimple," Carl said. He thought he'd had it all sewn up and wanted to go back to his hotel. Somehow I don't think Carl was one to wait around during celebrations, the part of the evening I looked forward to most.

"My experience with the technicians' union – in case you didn't know, sonny, I've been in a strike before," Larry was addressing Carl, "has led me to believe in commitment, in sticking to your union. If your union strikes then, by God, you strike. You support each other to a man. If we sign this we don't cross the picket line, see. You either stick by your union or you don't." As an afterthought Larry asked, "And how do I know who you are?"

Malcolm lifted his head, "Oh, come on. Look at the documents. We wouldn't. Never mind..." staring at the floor. Apparently, Larry wasn't worth talking to, even though we needed him.

"Look. If I sign I'm with the union. I don't go to work. You join a union; you stand by it."

"You do what the members tell you to do," Carl muttered. Larry wasn't listening.

"But then they'd find out what we've done!" Quixley said.

"Quixley, why don't you go get some beer," I said. "All we're going to do is apply, Larry. You can stick by the union later, when we're certified. When we *are* a union."

"Never mind the heroics," Malcolm couldn't keep out of this.

If Nate could have talked, he would have added a phrase like "quiet dignity" to these sentiments. But he couldn't talk.

"Iz very zimple," Carl said.

"We don't need you," Malcolm said. "But you better not fuck this up, Larry."

"Shut up!" Carl was speaking to Malcolm.

"Let the poor boy shit," Larry said. "I don't give a good goddamn. Who do you think you are, Carl? Carl the Kraut, ha ha."

"Come on, you guys," I said.

Laurie got up and walked out. As she went by I looked at her, angular in her skirt, almost gawky, wearing her dark nylons, and I felt a rush of tenderness. Nate seemed forlorn now that he had to sit by himself. No comment or gurgle was forthcoming to describe his loss, however. He was a real man.

"Never mind 'come on," Larry said. "Do we stick by a decision or not?"

"They'd just hire another staff," Carl said.

"And what about Quixley?" I added. "He signed on the understanding that he wouldn't lose his job. If they found out we'd all be suspended."

"Well, I don't like this mother here," Larry pulled a beer away from his lips and spewed at Carl. "A man should stand up." He calmed down quickly and started to pout, regarding the beer which he'd placed in his lap.

"Ah, come on, honey," Kitty said. Evidently Larry liked the phrase, he smiled. Malcolm remained quiet, but this head was up and he looked at Larry with glittering eyes. Except for his eyes his face was soft, almost blank with incredulity, and his mouth hung open slightly.

"Zis is ridiculous," Carl said.

Larry got up deliberately, then made a rush at Carl, making sure he passed in front of me so I could grab him. His arm was thin, tough as bristle.

"I've had enough of you!"

"Ze man is ridiculous!" Carl screamed.

Malcolm was on his feet; Nate was getting up saying "Hey, hey" in his big man's bass. Larry leaned out from me, I was using his arm like a leash, and shouted at Carl, "Where do you get off?"

"Don't be an asshole, Larry," Zeke sniffed, furtively wiping his nose.

Quixley was not in evidence.

Larry reached out with his free arm and grabbed at Carl's wig. He knocked it even more off balance but didn't pull it off. Carl grimaced. The thing must have been glued on. He took a step toward Larry, his round trunk seeming to swell with rage.

"Back off, mother, back off," Larry said. And although I still held his arm Larry somehow managed to get into a taunting, threating posture. He twisted to face Carl, his free hand low, making a fist.

"Fool," Carl puffed.

"Hey, hey," Nate said. I think he was really shocked.

Kitty sat dumb in the couch; her legs tucked up under her.

"Let's go," Malcolm said.

"You, you fucking goof." Larry turned on Malcolm. "Sitting there all night! You think a coma's a party joke?"

"Let's go, Carl," Malcolm said.

As Carl was smoothing himself out, though he'd hardly been ruffled, Larry punched him. Carl's swarthy, immaculate hands went to his face. Blood ran through his fingers. Malcolm shoved Larry hard, and Larry's arm jumped out of my grip, convulsing the way a deer's legs kick when it is dying. With an open palm Larry slapped Malcolm on the side of the face. "Let's go, you mother!" he roared. "Let's go!"

Suddenly Kitty was pulling at me, but I didn't have hold of Larry. Nate hovered like a helpless giant. Shaking his head, Zeke stayed seated. Then Malcolm tackled Larry and down they went.

I expected Kitty to scream "Stop them" but she just plucked tentatively at my shirt. Malcolm had Larry about the waist and was pushing, crawling with him across the floor. I pulled on Malcolm's hips; he was crawling like a baby with his rump high in the air. "Come on, let him go." With the pressure relaxed Larry continued to flail at Malcolm's back. The pounding was useless, Larry was smothered, and his fists cracked together. The forward movement began again, Malcolm crawling, holding Larry down with the pressure of his weight.

"For Chrissakes, quit it, Larry," I said. He lay still, Malcolm continuing to clutch his torso with both arms, the way a child clutches its mother's leg.

"Let him up," Zeke ordered.

Malcolm complied and Larry stood up, lean and proud.

"The little wire makes your average Pakistani look like a weightlifter," Malcolm said with contempt.

"Ah ha!" Larry pounced. He obviously thought he'd won the fight though Malcolm had thrown him to the floor as if he was a stick. Larry was built like a hemophiliac with a weight problem. "The big Marxist is a closet racist."

"Let's go, Carl," Malcolm said.

"Do you want to go again?" Larry twitched, as though he were going to step towards Malcolm and administer a backhand. "Outside?"

"Oh, for Chrissakes, Larry," I said. "He'd kill you."

"Come on, Carl, Nate," Malcolm said.

"Give me the fucking paper." Larry was addressing me.

"What? After all this you're going to sign?"

We were aghast. I looked at Carl who handed me one of the applications from his briefcase. The blood had smeared on his cheek, and a bright drop leaked from his nose.

Larry snatched the document, flourished it, and signed it.

"This doesn't mean I'm going to suckhole Nick or Pounder," he said. "I won't mention anything, but I think I can help the strike by working nights, and less effectively, from now on. That way I won't have to cross the picket line. But don't worry. I won't let on that we've applied for certification as a union. Quixley, all sucks, can rest assured."

"Good, that's good." Both Carl and Malcolm were happy. Nate farted. We were all in this together.

CHAPTER NINE

The winter came, and the wait began. Another job was out of the question because it would jeopardize my chances for reinstatement, or so I was told. It was about the only thing I was told.

At first I thought I wouldn't be able to stand it with nothing to do, but soon our life became a familiar one, and it was only when someone mentioned that April was the month for blizzards, when I looked ahead, that I fretted. But spring was a long way off, and I was sure the strike would be over by then.

We settled into a routine, the days as monotonous as the weather, the predictable shrinking daylight, the grey skies. Each morning I would pull the curtains and look up at a stain in the sky, a smear that matched the yellow colour of our lampshade. The lights in our apartment burned all day.

I'd make breakfast for Laurie, a late breakfast, and we'd listen to the CBC. She was both awkward, with her bouffant hair and bony white feet sticking out of her flannel nightgown, and graceful. We enjoyed being together, Laurie with her shy, remote smile, me fluttering from the coffee. The mornings were when we laughed most.

In the afternoon I'd go down to the library, or occasionally the union centre. I couldn't walk the picket line because I wasn't officially a member of the union, but I'd hang around stuffing envelopes and waiting for the news. There never was any. Larry followed his plan of working nights and kept his mouth shut; Zeke was subdued. Kitty returned to Muskeg.

At night I drank, but it wasn't the gulping, compulsive drinking of my first few months in Elk Brain. I had to do something while

Laurie was working, and the hotels offered me activity and a drab pageant. There were people to look at.

This drinking didn't make me sick, not sick with the insistent, debilitating hangovers I was used to. At 11 I'd leave the hotel, before the fights and the hard-edged alcoholic unhappiness, and go home to cook supper with a dazed, gently clumsy kind of drunk. I was ready to eat and sleep.

This couldn't go on, of course. It did go on. Months passed this way, and always I thought it'd be over soon. Slowly this thing was dragging me down, and I knew I had to change, something had to change. Nothing changed. And to think people lived years like this, locked into small towns and shopping and cooking and empty hours.

Christmas came and went. No news. I stayed in the apartment. The strike had to break. It didn't. Everyone went home for holidays and returned. I still didn't see much of Larry, but Zeke and Laurie and I would go out at least once a week and talk about change. Zeke was bored and fed up. The scenery, the weather, our expectant yet deadened state of mind never altered.

One night Laurie and I were drinking by ourselves at the Ironwood when I saw Big Bill Pounder at another table. I don't know why but Laurie had gotten dressed up. Perhaps she considered it was sort of a celebration. We had vaguely decided that if things didn't change in a couple of months we'd do something, anything: go back east, forget about this town and the strike and start something else. It used to excite me when Laurie looked like this, distant and whorish, hiding her long, small-breasted vulnerable body in her clothes. She was smoking and I was holding her hand and talking intensely. Suddenly I said, "I'm going over to say something to Pounder."

Laurie shrugged with the hard face she always used in bars.

Big Bill saw me coming, but he continued to talk to his companion, one of the managers the company had brought in to keep the *Tribune* running. They had kept it running in a reduced format.

"Excuse me, Bill. Can I have a word with you?"

"Sure, sure." He smiled, not moving, I was expected to have my word in front of the stranger. Bill stared smugly, pursed mouth, attentive. He was sharing a joke, but not with me.

"I just, I just, I just wanted to say that you said there'd be no repercussions and then I was fired. That same day. And I was told no repercussions." I was conscious of myself blushing.

Bill was perspiring, I could smell his shaving lotion. Light glanced off his eyes and off the glass ashtray on the table. His cigar was poised. "Okay, Randy, okay. You didn't come to work." He lifted his shoulders helplessly.

"You said no repercussions and you fired me. I might have come back to work." There were lines in Bill's big face, wrinkles round his eyes. His big glistening face had the sheen of a peeled potato.

My head was spinning. I was conscious of Laurie in the background, waiting in a cocktail dress with her purse tucked under her arm. She was like a figure in a Thirties frieze. This table I leaned over seemed the focus of the beverage room, but no one was paying attention. I looked at Big Bill, Bill the fat man. I could picture him stepping out of his jockey shorts for one of his dozens of showers, the apron of fat hanging over the band of his shorts. I could picture his future coronaries, his balance sheets, the way he looked in pajamas smoking a cigar. I felt no pity and no bitterness. As I walked away, I heard them both laughing behind my back.

CHAPTER TEN

Canadians are an indoor people. The shopping plazas, the bowling alleys, the Legion Hall and the beverage rooms of Elk Brain were full all winter. The streets were deserted. Shuffleboard flourished, cars were driven, heating bills rose. The cold was brittle, but the exhaust on Main Street gave the illusion of fog. The outskirts of town, the prairie, were a frozen sheet. Laurie and I had made up our minds to leave by spring, by early spring, if nothing broke regarding the strike. We were not unhappy.

In late January Larry was called away to visit his ailing mother. I'm not sure if that was the trip she died. Zeke had gone home for the weekend. Anyway Kitty, who had come to town on one of her periodic visits, was alone. Laurie and I went over to keep her company.

There was nothing to do that Friday night, especially as we had no transportation. Without Larry's car it would have been impossible to go the eight blocks to the hotel. We decided to spend the evening popping popcorn, drinking, and watching TV. The drinking was all right with me. I had lots of energy from my inactive day (when you're unemployed you're not exactly in the mood for cross-country skiing: it's enough to get up in the morning), but I didn't feel so trapped I had to get out. The walk over to Larry's had satisfied me. Besides, in Elk Brain one couldn't cross-country ski. At 30 below, one farmer's field alone would blind you, frostbite your skull, and kill you with tedium. The variations in the landscape aren't what you'd call picturesque. Plus, you can't buy the equipment. Hell, one monopoly restricted the kind of food we could get, the brand of soup. These merchants had no time for the decadence of skiing. What mattered was survival.

"I've got a casserole in the oven," Kitty said when she answered the door. She was dressed to kill, heels, her blond hair tossed like a cloud, wearing the white pant suit she'd worn the night I first met her. Kitty's perfume was an unsubtle brand and she'd painted her toenails and fingernails the same shade as her mouth. There was orange in her makeup, and the orange made the fine down on her face seem like fur.

I whistled. I always was quick and witty. "Lookin' good. Lookin' good."

"What are you all dolled up for?" Laurie wasn't prepared. She looked like a chorus girl on her day off, pancake makeup – I'm sure it was the same kind as Kitty's – a none too clean sweater and bell-bottom jeans that were too short for her. As a result her ankles stuck out of her pants like clappers on a bell. The jeans also made her seem high waisted, an effect that was not flattering to her bum.

"Why not?" Kitty answered Laurie. "It's Friday night."

"Goin' out steppin'?" Laurie imitated what I presume was the dialect of her native Muskeg. The girls laughed together.

"Have you guys eaten?" Kitty asked.

"What kind of casserole is it?" I replied.

"Tuna."

"We've eaten."

"We had some tea before we came," Laurie explained.

"Well, come on in," Kitty said. The Muskeg dialect surfaced again. "There's beer and vermouth in the fridge." Our hostess sashayed as we followed her. She seemed almost middle-aged with her big white behind and her high-heeled shoes, swinging her rump.

Our party was a quiet one until about 11. There wasn't much on TV but there was a lot of alcohol. I could hear the wood frame of the house creaking in the dry, brutal cold. We were cozy and crouched on the floor, huddled like street urchins over bowls of junk food and beer. The heat was turned up, the furnace consumed great amounts of fuel, and we were very warm.

When the news came on Laurie looked up. She could have been a chimpanzee the way she sat, ready to search for lice on Kitty or myself – social grooming.

"You know Randy and I are leaving Elk Brain this spring if nothing happens," she said. "We'll probably go back east."

"Well." Kitty arched her eyebrow and picked over a bowl of corn chips. "You and Randy," she repeated.

My reactions to this little exchange were various and subtle. On the one hand it was the first time Laurie had admitted in public that we were together, and I was very proud. On the other hand I resented Kitty's implication. Maybe she wasn't taking me seriously as a factor in Laurie's life. She knew about all the other men.

"So what's that supposed to mean?" I asked.

"What?" Kitty said innocently.

"Looking at Laurie like that." I had drunk a fair bit. In fact I'd even reverted to my old habits for the last hour or so and was gulping beer, waiting for an effect that never came. After about six the result is the same, no matter how many you swill.

"What are you talking about?" Kitty asked.

Laurie looked away, bored.

"Nothing. I'm just being paranoid and belligerent." I smiled.

"Who is this guy?" Kitty asked with vaudevillian puzzlement.

By now I'd forgotten my question. "Let's do something," I said.

"What?" Laurie asked.

"Laurie, you little street Arab you," I said.

"Do you know this guy?" Kitty could be almost as funny as Larry.

"We're having a party, aren't we?"

"Now he's going to say: 'Let's dance.'" Laurie was genial. It made me happy.

"I remember a party I went to as a kid, when I was about 12." Randy Gogarty was holding forth.

"Is that right?" Laurie Crawford was facetious.

"My dear," I said, "if I didn't idealize you, I'd think you were being rude. Anyway, we played a game called Life Story, or some kids' game like that. The girls made it up, but I remember it. Each person talked about themselves, told their secrets, in turn. Each person told their life story, you see."

"Thanks for explaining," Kitty said.

Undaunted, I continued. "I remember the thrill of being alone with girls all night in that dim apartment. Someone's parents were neglectful, thank God. They even had a picture of a pop-art penis in the bedroom. They were European, I think, and the old man was shady. I remember falling asleep with girls in the same room, the dim light, falling asleep.

"He's falling asleep," Kitty said. "So what is this? Life story?"

"How'd you meet Larry?" I asked her.

"I met him at the residence," Kitty said. "I was going with some other guy."

"Chuck." Laurie helped her along.

"Thanks. And Larry was standing there and he looked at me."

"You mean he looked at your ass," Laurie said.

"He was a cocky little bugger. He said he liked blondes. I knew who he was from his radio show."

"Since we're into party games," Laurie said, "let's play Mr. Dressup. I feel grungy in these clothes."

"You wanna wear something of mine?" Kitty asked.

"Sure. Why not?" They both looked at me with calculation. There was an intrigue here, and I couldn't figure it out.

"What did you do with those girls in the apartment, Gogarty?" Kitty had never called me by my last name before.

"Watched one of them fall asleep with her hand on her forehead, lying on her back. I could never figure out how she did it. I sleep on my side, in foetal position. It's because I'm not insecure."

The girls left in the middle of this explanation. They went to change. "Why are you doing this?" I yelled to them.

"Why not? We've done it before, and not for you."

I sat and pondered this remark, rather stupefied. Turning off the TV, I hollered, "We're almost out of ale."

"Then get the vermouth," Kitty answered with a shout.

I knew that once we started on the vermouth we'd be sick the next day, guaranteed, but I didn't bother to relay this information. Kitty was in there preparing the bride. I was getting to the stage when I'd drink the water out of a flower vase if I thought it contained alcohol. In fact, once, at precisely this stage of inebriation, I had tried it. Laurie'd urged me on. She likes a drink herself occasionally. This was the stage when I start to empty other people's drinks when they leave for the washroom. It's a favourite trick of mine in nightclubs. I'm a cunning bastard.

The parade began. Kitty returned in a silk bathrobe with Larry's initials monogrammed on the lapel; Laurie affected a pant suit that didn't fit. A chiffon scarf had been tied in the belt loops. Laurie also wore Kitty's clogs and they were much too small for her. They stuck on the end of her toes like little caps. The two of them were vulgar and touching. They were doing this for me!

"What is this?" I asked. "A wife swap in Don Mills?"

Like two sisters playing house, hands on hips, necks stretched thin and haughty, they actually modelled for poor old Randy Gogarty. Kitty broke the spell. "Where the fuck is Don Mills? And what does this have to do with wives?"

"Don Mills is in Toronto, angel. And it's ugly. It makes shopping out here at the Bi-Rite," I gestured, "seem like an orgy. As for wives: I feel like a policeman or bank manager at a swap. Only there's no one to swap with. It's that sorta atmosphere, the two of you putting on a show."

The girls bent their knees, sloped their shoulders and posed. They had the perfect bad posture of models. They turned around, the freshly applied perfume spun off them, and their lip gloss shone.

"Ever been to a 'swap'?'" Laurie asked.

"Nope."

The fashion plates collapsed onto the floor, sitting cross-legged like Girl Guides. They each took a swig of vermouth from the bottle. A giggle would have been appropriate but was not forthcoming. The girls looked at each other and nodded in a burlesque of mutual consent. "Let's get Gogarty."

"Wait a minute. Wait a minute," I said. "I've never done anything like this. You mean with the two of you?"

They further agreed. "Don't you think it'll do him good, Kitty?" Laurie said.

"Yes."

"I'm not sure I believe in it," I said, hoping against hope they'd continue.

"Please don't throw me in the briar patch." Kitty was gleeful.

"We'll be sick," I said.

They continued to regard each other with a kind of piercing, jolly anticipation.

"I'm glad you understand each other." I said.

"You go into the bedroom," Laurie said.

"I don't believe in this but…"

"Let's get Gogarty."

I'll beat them at their own game, I thought, as I went into Larry's bedroom and took off my clothes. They won't expect to find me like this.

The ladies kept me waiting and I could hear water running, doors closing, toilets flushing, and lights being turned off before Kitty came into the room. I had been sitting on the bed's edge and I stood up. "Oh my," she said when she saw I was naked, flattering me with a whisper. Kitty opened her robe and stepped out of it.

Her breasts were large, her body full and golden. She walked right by me, the fat of her buttocks over-compacted and dimpled. I reached out and brushed her stomach as she passed, hard as a gourd under the velvet skin. Kitty was demure and clean, with sweet tiny feet and hands. In contrast her hair was coarse and lush and womanly. She quickly got under the covers.

"Where's Laurie?" I asked.

Kitty just looked at me, a little girl who wanted to sleep. She raised her hand and rested the back of it on her forehead.

"What's the matter? Got a headache?" I walked over to her.

With her eyes half closed she reached out and began to fondle my cock and balls. Cupping the turgid penis she raised it to her mouth. Kitty closed her eyes completely; her mouth was as wet and soft as a baby's.

Now Laurie showed up. She was wearing a nightgown and I turned to look at her as Kitty held me in her mouth. "Why are you wearing that?" I asked.

"My, my," Laurie said and lifted the gown over her head.

"Why'd you even put it on?" The gown had accented the flatness of her body, her nipples were like blue bruises under the silk.

Kitty stopped caressing me. "He's very bold," she said. "When I got here he was naked."

"Ummm." Laurie walked by me and got into bed. I was left standing, afraid to move because I knew my cock would bob all over the fucking place if I did.

"So, what do we do now?".

I needn't have bothered to ask. Laurie leaned over and pulled Kitty towards her. They kissed.

"Wait a minute. Wait a minute. Let me in on this." I got into bed with them.

Crawling between the lovers I broke their embrace and lay down. Laurie continued to admire Kitty and stroked her hair. The booze I'd drunk was beginning to have its effect and the room started to come at me in waves. The poison was taking hold. The girls were at it again over my corpse. They ran their hands down my body, reaching my balls, taking turns lifting, judging them. Then they lay back.

Who first? What a choice. Kitty was perfumed and heavy, her eyes closed, her mouth pursed, expectant. Laurie was as angular as a brother. Her legs were rough, her clay cold body familiar, unwashed.

I chose Laurie. It wasn't duty and it wasn't desire. It's just that Laurie took chances. Unlike Kitty or Birdwell or any of the other women I knew, she didn't play it safe. In spite of all her passivity and all the men, in spite of her silences and the air of dead mystery, she seemed to risk something. I loved her for it.

Laurie's thighs opened and I could feel the V of tendons where her legs met her body; I could feel her hollow belly, her flat breasts. Lifting her rump I mounted my girl and pumped her, pumped the stink and musk of her groin. Laurie's mouth was hard. She cried out, squeezed me with her legs, thrust up and hurt me with her pelvis. Immediately I turned to Kitty. I don't know how I managed it; I wasn't taking any coffee breaks. Kitty was soft. Her plump rich body seemed to gurgle and she said, "Uh." I don't remember much after that. The three of us were warm and dark, and I pulled the covers over my head. The night pressed cold at the window.

The sun woke me early, and I knew I'd be sick all day. But the soft nausea hadn't reached me yet, it just promised to come. I trembled. The light could have been spring light.

Laurie was facing me, hair greasy, with a little stain on the pillow where she was breathing. Her eyelids were pale as the sky. Kitty was turned the other way, her hair in a golden crumpled heap. It wasn't supposed to be this way at all. I'd never felt so safe. We were as close as children.

CHAPTER ELEVEN

"We gotta do something."

Zeke and Larry, Kitty, Laurie and I were sitting around in the middle of the bleakest winter I'd ever experienced. The sky was the colour of jaundice, the beer was the colour of jaundice and the cold unbelievable. We had nothing to do, no work we cared about, no winter sport and not enough money. Our major adventure had been an expedition to the shopping centre to purchase a barbecue. Larry thought it'd be a lark if we barbecued in the backyard, at 30 below. The aim was to get the steaks back inside the house before they froze. At least it'd be a switch, he said. He wanted to try it.

We gave up on this plan after Larry touched the grate bare-handed and lost the skin off his fingertips. This was the social event for January. I didn't know I could be so unhappy.

The union told us nothing about what was going on. One afternoon as I was stuffing envelopes a fellow stuffer let it drop that the certification bid had failed. The newsroom staff was just not large enough to form a union; it was that simple. I confronted Malcolm with this, and he said not to worry. After the strike we'd get more help and try again: after the strike.

"And the case for your reinstatement is going up before the Saskatchewan Labour Board." Malcolm wanted to make it up to me with the gift of information.

"When?"

"You'll be called on to appear. You could win a lot of back pay."

"What about representation? What about a lawyer? Where's Carl?"

"Don't worry. We'll arrange everything. You'll be called on to appear."

This was the reason I stuck around, and it wasn't much of a reason. But where could I go? I was convinced there was no way out of Elk Brain in the winter. In fact, I knew there were no buses, cars, trains. How could anyone live out there? They'd die of boredom. The only realities were the tiny endless repetitive meals in our apartment, the landscape from a window, the books and meetings with my friends. Besides, if I did get a judgement in my favour at the Labour Board Laurie and I could really escape.

Life at the *Tribune* went on much as before, or so I was told. If the management had found out about our attempt to form a union, they didn't let on. Zeke slouched around with what he considered bad assignments, Larry did his night stint, Quixley continued to work long hours and to dip his hands in vats of chemicals when he developed his photos, raising these same hands to a face that continued to break out.

Needless to say the captivity had taken the bloom off my honeymoon with Laurie. But then, maybe she was used to this sort of season, having been born in it. She kept on supporting us by waitressing at the Holiday Inn, and some nights she didn't get home until very late. I never questioned her about it. She always came home.

The most distressing thing was our indifference. If you think this was a turnaround, especially on my part, try spending a winter with another person in one room. St. Francis of Assisi, the effeminate bastard, would drive you up the wall. Try spending a winter with another person in Elk Brain. In a situation like this, indifference isn't malignant.

A newer and more disturbing element entered our lives. It wasn't what Laurie did late at night, and her ex-boyfriend, the

Satanist weasel of Muskeg, didn't come and kidnap her. Its just that she came to repulse me.

That's a strong word, so I'll explain. One morning I saw her naked and the sight made me want to leave the apartment, get out, escape. She had gone into the kitchen and was reaching up to get some sugar out of the cupboard. The light was harsh, illuminated every line on her body. In spite of her long frame she had stretch marks all over! O God, I'm a sick bastard, but it made me angry. I felt betrayed and bored. Boredom can be the other side of adoration.

Now don't get me wrong. If she'd made a move to leave, I'd have freaked out. When she got dressed to go to work, her purse tucked under her arm like a beautiful whore, looking coarse and chic at the same time, I knew how much I needed her. I did not have to be reminded that she was the first woman I'd lived with. With tensions like these between us is it any wonder we'd agree to almost anything for relief and amusement.

"We gotta do something."

"Do what?" Laurie asked, always the cynic.

Zeke smiled ruefully. His nose seemed to be afflicted with permanent frostbite; with a tip like that, he was beginning to look like Pinocchio.

"Go for a picnic," old One Lung replied. Even Larry seemed tired and sighed his idea out. Usually he'd have been semi-screaming or cracking his wizened features with a grin.

"Oh, Larry," Kitty elbowed him. "You're funny. What about the barbecue?"

"Yeah! What about the barbecue?" This was the closest I'd ever seen Zeke to belligerence. He was fast on the uptake, Zeke was.

"Don't be sulky." Kitty was defending her man and taking Zeke's balls off. Her tone was that of: "Don't be a sucky baby." My, we were a discontented lot.

Randy Gogarty sat silent, filled with a bitter self-pity. I was concentrating on my latest obsession. You see, I was sure I was getting tannic acid poisoning from drinking too much tea. My body felt one with the cushion I sat on. Flab is another feature of the Canadian north. My partner in common-law, Miss Crawford, also said nothing. I think we were feeling the winter worst of all. She was dressed for a nightclub.

"This is different," says Larry. "We'll go out to Buffalo Pound Park with a couple of bottles and a lunch. We can eat in the car and scare the shit out of those bastards."

"What bastards?" I roused myself out of an irritated somnolence.

"The buffalo, asshole. The warden feeds them every morning – they're on welfare – then he takes off. The bastards are fat as turds. Maybe we can run a little of the fat off the bastards, eh? We'll have the place to ourselves, we can have a look around. Nobody'll be out there."

"'Cause nobody can step outside a car and live," I said.

"Don't be a suck, man."

"What about skiers?" Zeke asked. "Isn't there a ski trail in the park. And the downhill area isn't far away."

"Nobody used the trail, man. And the downhill area's miles away. We'll have the buffalo all to ourselves."

"I'd like to see them," I said.

"You're fucking right. We can sneak right up on them like the Indians did."

"What'd ya mean?" My mood was transformed. As a kid in Toronto I'd devoured animal stories, Ernest Thompson Seton, Charles G.D. Roberts. These tales had inspired me, and a less imaginative though much tougher friend from Cape Breton. We formed a wolf pack and ran down other children in relays, the way I read that wolves ran down deer. Instead of hamstringing our victims we merely exhausted them and pushed them around. We also went hunting. My buddy would climb up under the railway bridge and throw down parasite-ridden squabs which I caught in my windbreaker. These squabs were then fed to his dog, a part beagle who soon learned to anticipate the hideous little monsters. I remember they leaked a substance like egg yolk when killed.

Well, all this prepared me for the wilderness, though my wilderness had been train tracks. I knew about hunting, though most of my adolescence had been spent south of Bloor Street. "Will we hide in robes and pretend we're other buffalo?" I asked. "Or should we get wolf skins?"

I'm very excitable. Laurie dangled her wedgies; I was being stupid again. To avenge myself I thought how easy she'd be to track with feet as big as hers.

"We'll just hop the fence and go after the buggers," Larry said. "Run 'em to death, ha, ha!" He was coming to life.

In spite of torturing animals regularly as a child I am ecologically minded. In fact, I broke with my friend after he hammered a mature pigeon with 82 BBs. "I don't want to hurt them," I said.

"Man, don't be a suck. Hurt them!" he said with disgust.

Larry had used the word suck too often. I was thinking what it'd be like to punch him out.

"I've got Thursday off," Laurie said, rescuing Larry.

"Let's all go!" we said in unison.

Thursday came, and on a cloudy inert morning we set off. Mist hung in the air, which was strange for Elk Brain. One could have been fooled into thinking it was humid, but the cold was bitter.

Once we left town the prairie asserted itself. The highway past the shopping plaza crested a hill and the landscape appeared. I'd been huddled in a room so long I was frightened. To avoid the fields, the emptiness, I had to stare at the side of the road. Jagged stalks of wheat broke through the snow. The horizons were so far away, but once I got used to them, reassuring. The streaks of cloud and weather in the distance couldn't hurt me.

The girls sat bundled in the back seat, hunched and sullen. They wore skirts, not very appropriate stalking gear in my opinion, and tuques. Everyone was smoking and breathing each other's breath. The heater was on full blast and Larry wouldn't turn it down. He sat at the wheel in a sport coat, and his lack of sleep was beginning to show. He was hardly voluble. It could have been a Sunday drive, and father was a cranky midget.

The park wasn't far away, and we reached it in half an hour. Our chauffeur pointed out that he had been right: the toll booths were deserted, and he gunned up to them. Blowing snow curled around the concrete foundations. Paint was flaking in the frost.

"So, where is it?" I asked. "The Buffalo Pound?"

"I don't know." Larry indicated he had the responsibility of driving. "Why don't you get out and look."

I supposed a big board crusted with snow was a map of the park and went to examine it. Outside, the cold made me nervous. Even though we were in a little hollow the wind blew, and I thought the leaden sky could mean a blizzard. We had seen no other cars on the way out.

Breaking the crust I saw two very faint lines branching off from an arrow that read: "You are here." There were little smudges representing buffalo on either side of the lines. The map could have been a rock painting with its crude representations of animals and vein-like tracings.

"There are two routes you can take," I said when I rejoined my friends, adding to their irritation by my breathlessness. "I don't think it matters which we choose. They both circle back here and they both have buffalo drawn on each side of them."

"Okay. Let's get the bastards."

"Anyone want a sandwich?" Kitty asked.

No one wanted a sandwich.

We did not see any buffalo. Bald mounds of unbroken snow rose up on either side of us as we descended into the hollow. The sky wasn't flat and stretching anymore. We were trapped. Wire mesh fence followed each side of the road.

"There they are!" I cried, spotting two brown mounds on one of the hillocks. The buffalo must have been facing away from us. The humps of their backs were blurred, half covered by blowing snow.

My companions didn't seem interested, but Laurie rubbed away the steam on her window to peer out. Suddenly I was very proud. My early training as a woodsman had proved me fit.

"Oh yes," my girlfriend said, "there they are."

Larry pushed up his sleeves and kept on driving. Father had taken the wrong turn and didn't want to admit it.

"We came all this way for that?" Kitty said. Zeke rubbed his nose with the back of his hand, sniffed, and looked out.

Why didn't they realize how strange it was to see the buffalo up there, the only colour in the drift and snow?

"Let's have a closer look," I said.

"Goddamn right," Larry said, "we're going after them."

"Don't be cwazy." Kitty could have been hugging a teddy bear.

"Goddamn right." Larry pulled up. As he rolled down his sleeves, he squinted out the window, wrinkling his monkey face to let us know he was judging the distance, the day, and the tactics we'd use to approach the beasts. As he reached his conclusions he exhaled, "Okay."

"Come on!" Zeke said. "We can't go out there."

"Well, let's at least have a look at them," I said. "Maybe they're musk ox. They could be in an environment like this."

"You're cwazy," Kitty said. "I'm not moving."

"You stay here if you want, honey," Larry's voice indulged and soothed. "But those bastards are going to know we're here." He stated the inevitable.

"You're cwazy." Kitty cuddled up to her regression. The rest of us got out of the car.

Again I had a disquieting sense of isolation. It wasn't overpowering. I just felt anxious and slightly hollow. There was nothing but the road, the sky, the muffled hills. With a combination of boredom and reluctance I stepped away from the vehicle. The wind blew. I wanted to get back inside where it was claustrophobic and familiar. "Surely they can't be grazing?" I said.

Everyone turned their heads to look at me as if I was an idiot. The trouble was they were serious. Larry started toward the fence.

"Let's not," I wailed. "Buffalos are big animals." My cowardice was not a hit. Larry began climbing. Laurie had wandered up the road a bit and turned to follow him. She looked like a Russian in her tall boots, and for some reason I had notions of love in the snow. Zeke waded after them, sifting through the drifts. The snow was granular as sand.

"I wonder why there isn't any crust on this stuff," I shouted, following. The fence wasn't a high one and I managed to get over it easily.

"Listen to the great hunter," Larry said, already starting up the hill. He tossed further insults over his shoulder. "Those are fuckin' cows, man. We'll be lucky to get close to them before they run."

We began to get close to them and they didn't run. Their backs faced us and stayed buried in the snow. I thought I felt vegetation underfoot as we walked, bent in a mat over the hard ground, but it was difficult to tell. Occasionally we sank, though not very deeply. I wondered if Laurie's boots were adequate. She was wearing tights so I guess I needn't have worried. I was trying to think about her thighs.

We'd covered a fair distance when I stopped and turned around. The others kept on. It seemed I was looking down on the car from a great height. I'd lost contact with it, and the hill opposite loomed closer. Its snowfields were as empty as the ones we were on. These people had lived out here all their lives; they must have known what they were doing.

My steel spectacles cut into my head, my skull felt like it was contracting from the cold. I had a sudden sharp pain in my forehead. God, I needed a hat. I trudged after my friends.

Our quarry didn't grow in size as we approached. The buffalo, or cows, were no threat, half covered by swirling snow.

Larry reached them first. "Freezer beef," he called back, kicking at the patch of brown in front of him.

"You mean they're dead!" I shouted.

Obviously, I didn't deserve an answer. Laurie and Zeke gathered round the chief scout while I straggled up.

"Are they cattle or not?" I asked. It was a legitimate question. Larry kicked a shaggy hide. Snow bounced up like dust. The buffalo were dead, with only their humps visible. They must have died kneeling, the rest of their bodies were covered, locked into the earth.

"Frozen solid," Laurie said redundantly. The cold had affected her makeup, turning it bright orange. Zeke's nose looked sore.

"I wonder how these two got cut off from the herd?" He pushed at the carcass with his foot. There was no give in it.

"Well, there's plenty more where they came from," and Larry grimaced to make his skin leathery. In his case it wasn't difficult to do. "I wonder what's over that rise." He squinted up the slope.

"Yonder?" I pointed. Nobody saw the joke, let alone paid me any attention. I didn't want to look at the buffalo hides, stiff as frozen rugs.

The hill opposite was featureless and the road was far below. I could barely make out the fences, but I saw exhaust rising from the car and was glad Kitty had kept it running.

Larry started to climb again, and Laurie jogged after him. She ran with that graceful, almost bounding, way of running women athletes have, her elbows pointed away from her body. Zeke looked at me quizzically.

"Let's go," I said and pivoted into the wind. Another headache cracked in my skull. I pinched the skin of my forehead into a furrow to relieve it.

As Larry disappeared over the ridge Laurie stopped. I could see her from the waist up. Zeke and I ran to catch them, our lungs hurting from the cold.

Leaping through the drifts, waving his arms and shouting, One Lung Larry Brennen ran toward six buffalo who faced him in the valley. They were bunched together in a dirty yard, unmoving. An open shed stood to the left, and the bowl of the hills surrounding them was blank.

"Yahoo!" Brennen shouted. I almost thought he was in slow motion the way he splashed, drove through the drifts, but his arms were frantic. The three of us posed at the top of the hill, grim as monuments.

Straw and urine had coloured the snow in the yard yellow, and the animals had cut up mud and droppings with their hooves, churning them into paste. One big bull lowered his head, cocking it to one side. The hump of muscle and fat on his back seemed to wiggle.

"Yahoo," Larry's voice was fainter. He ran on.

"Larry!" I yelled. Laurie was impassive, but her eyes narrowed. My snow queen's face was grey as slate.

He crumbled. It wasn't like TV, or movies; there was no instant replay, no slow motion. He crumbled without grace or heaviness. It was as instant as a punch in the face.

The three of us launched ourselves toward him like skiers starting down a hill. It was a jarring, dangerous run. Zeke got there first. Larry lay face down in the snow.

"Larry!" He didn't move.

"Larry!" I rolled him over. Snow crystals clung to his face, his moustache, his open eyes.

"The buffalo!" Laurie shook me. They had formed a half circle and were moving toward us, not 20 yards away.

"Scare them off." I put my mouth over Larry's, remembering to tilt his head back. His mouth was open over his teeth, and his teeth were as wet and glassy as his eyes.

I blew into him, covering his nose. Nothing happened. His chest didn't rise. Zeke and Laurie were holding hands and walking toward the buffalo. "Go away," they said. "Go away now." They moved their free arms up and down like semaphores. The beasts stopped; they were reluctant to leave their yard.

Larry was not breathing. My eyeballs hurt from trying to look at Zeke and Laurie while I gave artificial respiration. I shut my eyes and blew. Larry's cheeks ballooned, but his chest didn't move. His moustache and even his skin were bristly as I covered his mouth with mine. I pinched both nostrils hard and his head seemed to roll as I held him by the nose.

"What's the matter?" Kitty was kneeling beside me.

How did she get here? I glanced up. The top of her tuque had fallen forward and the stringed-tassel dangled and bobbed before her eyes.

Zeke and Laurie had returned. I could feel them standing above me. Still I concentrated on what I was doing. This close to the ground I could see the separate snow crystals, and I was conscious of the texture of Larry's skin, the way the hairs grew out of his face.

"Let me try," Zeke said. It was as if we were trying to fix a flat tire, a bunch of friends standing around, helpless and impatient. The surprise of when it happened, when we'd all been calm and rushed to help, was over. Now we were inconvenienced and helpless.

"Just a minute!" I resented being interfered with.

"Larry!" Kitty grabbed the sleeve of his ski jacket and shook. The arm was as limp and mocking as a rag doll's.

Was his chest tight? I hammered it with my fist.

"Larry!" Kitty hit him, slapped his grimacing face. Part of her hand struck me on the cheek.

"Here." Zeke knelt down and I moved out of the way. It was no use; I hoped Zeke would fail. Here Larry was dead, and I was worried about my competence. We were waiting, action was finished, and I put my hand on Kitty's shoulder. The sky was still, my knees were wet.

"I thought something had happened!" Kitty began to sob. Thank God she was crying. It was a reaction we could expect and Zeke, Laurie and I were silently respectful.

"Get him to the car!" Kitty shook Larry again. There was something we could do. "Get him to the car!" she said.

The stillness of the afternoon disappeared as I helped lift Larry and put him across Zeke's shoulders. We ran back up the hill, Larry jostling across Zeke's back. I hoped Larry'd get hurt; I wanted Zeke to be rougher with him. Maybe he'd wake up.

The wind hit us when we were out of the hollow. Our clothing rustled, we gasped, the snow shifted and blew as we pushed through it. The rush and noise were comforting.

"Did you leave the car running?" I asked Kitty.

"Yes," she panted.

Good, I thought. We'll get out of here.

We put Larry in the back seat, between Kitty and me. He didn't seem like a corpse, at least I didn't notice if his eyes were open, and I had a sense of elation. He'd be all right.

Then Kitty sat him up. His leg flopped across her thigh. Larry was propped against her like a ventriloquist's dummy. His eyes were wide.

"Lay him down," I said. She pushed at his face until it was buried in her lap. Kitty was crying. The tassel of her tuque continued to bob and dangle in front of her. Blond hair spilled out of the hat.

"Hurry," I said, though Zeke had started to drive. "We can turn around and go back the way we came."

"I know. That's what I'm doing." The car began to fog up and Zeke turned on the defroster. Everything was a shade of grey: the moisture on the windows, the blank hills, the fences breaking through the drifts, what sky one could see out the windshield. Snow was beginning to fall.

"Where's the turn?" Zeke asked Laurie. She sat straight beside him in the front seat. Her seriousness almost amounted to rigidity, but a shadow of concern twisted her face, lips set, eyebrows furrowed.

"There. Up ahead," she said. I didn't bother to look but continued to stare out the window. The car swerved.

"You know where the hospital is." Kitty said. It was an order, not a question.

"Yes." We were on the prairie now, and the flatness was a relief from the bowl we'd just escaped. There were patches of brown in the fields, and the snow blew past us, thinned by the wind and our speed.

What had happened to Larry? I couldn't ask. We were quiet, and I felt I was choking on the humidity in the car, smothering on my own breath. Flinching, I wondered if Larry was touching me, but his torso lay across Kitty and his legs were on the floor. He could have been sleeping, though people didn't sleep sprawled like that. Zeke wiped the windshield with his mitt.

"His lung collapsed," Kitty said, not addressing any of us. "His lung collapsed."

I turned to them. Larry lay like a child hiding in mum's lap, but he was so loose. His body moved with the motion of the vehicle.

"He could be breathing very slightly," I said. Maybe I should have shut up, and I didn't want her to turn him over, but we had to say something to each other.

"Yeah." Zeke let it be known he was concentrating on driving.

"He's only got one lung. The left lung collapsed four times. Four times. They peeled it, they peeled it. They had to remove it. They took it out. Now..."

His right lung had collapsed. Kitty was making herself cry, making herself explain. It was better than just sitting there. Laurie twisted around. She bit her lips and nodded at Kitty.

Zeke was pulling us over to the shoulder.

"What's the matter?" I asked.

"The sign back there said Tooley. I must have turned the wrong way when we came out of the park."

"Turn around!" Kitty didn't have to tell him. It didn't matter. We reached the hospital in an hour.

Kitty and I left Larry face down on the back seat and ran into emergency. "Can't breathe. In the car."

We were attended very quickly. The receptionist hurried out of the room and returned with an intern. He was carrying a small cylinder of oxygen.

"In the car!" Kitty exclaimed.

I held back for a moment. There were no other patients in emergency, and the room was very still, as still and empty as the streets of Elk Brain on the drive in. When I did go out to the car the doctor had turned Larry over and was holding the oxygen mask to his face. Laurie and Zeke were not watching.

It was too late. Larry was turning blue. The mask was left on when they put Larry on a stretcher. Before he was wheeled away Kitty pulled his boots off, I don't know why. The mask covered Lar's face but I could see his eyes, staring incredulous, blank. His forehead was furrowed with outrage and glee.

They took him away with his feet sticking out of the blankets. His socks were rolled down and exposed his ankles, bony and frail.

CHAPTER TWELVE

Larry's death was a blessing for the management of the *Tribune*, and they acted upon it. Nick did his job; they could save money that way, and I was replaced by the son of a company man, a sloppy-fat, loud-mouthed 20-year-old who made his father seem like a radical. With this bully in the office there'd never be any hope for a newsroom union, no matter how the strike went. I'd been purged and Zeke had finally quit. I'm not sure he gave notice, or even told anyone; he just disappeared and went back to his parents. God help him – winter on a farm in norther Saskatchewan with his old man walking around and looking at Zeke with concern. Mother intervening. At least the old hunky would have something to keep him interested; with Zeke to worry about he could feel superior, act compassionate and have family conferences. A little disgust would help his retirement along. Superiority is good for the aged.

The last time Laurie and I saw Zeke was at the funeral home. The undertaker had convinced Larry's mother that hanging around in Elk Brain in an open coffin would be good for her boy before he was shipped home for burial. Give his friends a chance for a few words of goodbye. As old Lar had said so often, his mother was "full of cancer," so I guess she wasn't too hard to convince. She returned to her hospital bed and Larry remained with us. Respects were to be paid.

The funeral parlour had been recently renovated. There were white walls, mock oak beams, and a bright red rug. It wasn't unlike a cocktail lounge with the subdued lighting, lots of red, drapes. I'd occasionally picked up funeral notices for the paper at the front door of this place when I was working. They were so common, a regular feature of the *Tribune*, that it was a bit of a surprise to find out what they actually meant.

Larry was too small for his coffin. Oh, the coffin was magnificent (that is, it cost a lot), his features were tranquil, and his hands folded. But he was too small for it. He was also not alone. Another member of the numberless legions shared this converted house with him, a Mrs. Titswilly. She was laid out in an adjoining room that was separated from Larry's by a folding wall. Larry had few flowers; Mrs. Titswilly too many. I took a peek at her before Laurie and I went in to see our friend.

There had been no funeral director to greet us at the door. Mrs. Titswilly lacked mourners and so did Larry Brennen. Laurie and I had the whole place to ourselves.

"Don't he look lovely now, the old devil."

Laurie approved this corniness, glancing at me out of the corner of her eye as she signed the guest book.

"Where is everyone?" she asked.

"No Nick. No Pounder. No Kitty. I guess if they were here it was earlier. No wreath from the *Tribune,* you notice."

"We didn't send a wreath."

"We didn't have to."

Then Zeke joined us. We hadn't heard him approach. He wiped his hand across his nose, looked back the way he'd come, and said in one breath, "Hi, I've quit."

"That's too bad."

"Yeah."

"This whole thing is a mess," I said, thinking of myself, of Zeke, of the egotism of the living. "Let's have a look." We approached the display.

My buddy had been sewn. I could see some sort of thread up his nose. Lar was so calm and empty, so unlike himself. His hands were clean, and rigid, so rigid when I touched them, with just a tiny rubber-like give. Makeup couldn't completely hide the blue, and for all the creamy smoothness with it had been applied, the rouge on Larry's cheeks looked powdery. He was cold. I was shocked by the obviousness. He was cold.

"He doesn't know we're here," Zeke said sadly. It was not meant as a joke.

"Umm." Larry didn't know we were here, I was thinking slowly. Laurie had stayed away.

"Can I help you?" I turned to find Mr. Dotswold Goan, the undertaker, staring over my left shoulder at his work. The teetotaler had bad breath.

"Oh, hello," I said. "It's a shame about Larry."

"I'm sure the deceased would have appreciated your visit."

I knew Goan. He was the last guy I'd tried to interview on council before the strike. I'd had a few beers with Malcolm, and went to the meeting lit. My radio announcer colleague had not been very friendly, and Goan even less so. Blurting out something about beer and the strike I had fouled up.

"You did a fine job," Zeke said. Again he was not trying to be funny.

"Yeah. It's too bad," I said, meaning about Larry, of course.

"We do our best." Goan's eyes glittered. He knew my name but he wasn't going to use it. Oh, I knew Goan all right. His family had been members of Elk Brain's governing body for two generations. The particular representative in front of me was second generation. Since the Goans were no longer nouveau riche you'd have thought Dotswold could afford dentures that fit. But no, the pair that clicked at me were interchangeable with Tinkus Dixford's, as was the smile.

"Well, I guess we gotta go," I said. Laurie was waiting in the background. Normally I'd have thought her sexy, posed against a curtain in high heels with her purse tucked under her arm. Now she just seemed attractive. She's a good kid, I thought. Laurie was not perky, or ready to kid or comfort me; yet I looked toward her expecting an emotional cheerleader. Mixed up with this was the exact feeling I had when relatives gathered. I had to get out. The three of us had been in the chapel 10 minutes, and the last two felt like two hours of a family dinner. The same expectations were present. I had to get out.

"You've had the place redone, I see," Zeke said. Good old Zeke, he knew what to say. "It reminds me of the Ironwood." Zeke did not know what to say. Temperance fiend Goan fawned and smiled and hated.

"I believe it was the same decorator."

Decorator! The only decorator in Elk Brain was a hairdresser who doubled as a carpenter. This palace had been designed by a mining engineer on his day off.

"Is your lab in the basement?" I asked. I thought of Larry lying on a stretcher in a white room with closed cupboards all over the wall. The room was the size of a big domestic lavatory.

"Why it's in the back, off the garage." Goan, the man of science, was delighted by my interest, though neither of us mentioned embalming. Next he was going to tell me how his wife used coffin lining to line her dresses. It was his favourite story, involving both the saving of money and the mention of his business. I'd heard it at the chamber of commerce three times, in the days I wasn't a pariah. "Can I help you further?"

How about a tour? was on my lips but Laurie dragged me away.

"Has Mr. Pounder been down?" Zeke asked.

"I can't say."

140

"You don't know, eh?"

"Can I help you further?" We were being asked to leave. Who needed his little rat trap of a funeral home anyway? Larry certainly wasn't inside.

"Well, goodbye," Laurie said.

I glared, angry at Laurie, and her background, for seeming to respect this lank-framed, loose-suited bugger. Goan would go on making speeches about service in the community, go on installing rugs that were easy to sneak around on, go on passing laws to repress much of life in this town, and people would respect him for it. Grudgingly, without a thought on Saturday night, they'd respect him because he was one of them.

The usually diffident Zeke said nothing. I was glad we were allies in our dislike of this caricature. Goan reminded me of what Zeke used to call, glancing away, "the English." Actually, he was my idea of a Scots Presbyterian. Whatever he may have been I certainly wouldn't want to ask him for a loan. Goan was Canadian, and like most of our architecture, and history, Victorian.

"See you around," I said. It irked me that we'd been kicked out.

Zeke said goodbye on the street, and that was the last we saw of him. He walked across the municipal park, turning by the steam locomotive to wave. Snow had begun to fall, and Zeke's checkered pants were bright in the grey. He'd been saying for a long time he was fed up, but it was the only hint we had. He must have left that afternoon.

"How about some Chinese food?" I asked Laurie. The day stretched ahead interminably. Every day stretched ahead interminably. It was always Sunday with nothing to do and now the snow had started again.

"All right," she said. "But let's go to the Polynesian Village. I don't want to walk too far. My feet are beginning to kill me."

That's what we lived with for the next month, Laurie's worsening feet – bunions and corns and bleeding callouses on a 21-year-old – the absence of friends and time. I stopped going to the union hall. I stopped drinking. Middle age hit. Days were spent lying around the overheated apartment in my underwear. I enjoyed flatulence, self-indulgence, sleeping with Laurie but not making love to her. I masturbated every chance I had. When alone I would make my stomach protrude over my undies, fat and white and round, and look in the mirror. I developed piles. Laurie lost her job because of her feet. We lay around together. The windows fogged up, the oven was always on and we read a lot. Then the call to battle came.

"Can you make it to the Chateau Prairie in Regina tomorrow?" Malcolm McSweeney said.

"Why, Malcolm?" I had a headache and was thinking of two more aspirins, a pot of tea and some bake-it-yourself puff pastries.

"Your case has come up before the Labour Board. The hearing is tomorrow."

Months of sameness had led to this!

"Fill me in, you fucking asshole. What about a lawyer? What am I supposed to say? Who'll be there?"

"Just show up."

"Fuck off. What time did you say?"

"Nine o'clock."

The money was important. Reinstatement, or back pay, would mean a big difference in our lives. Insecurity about our fate caused Laurie and I to go out and get pissed, our first celebration in ages. We wrapped up warmly and waddled down to the Ironwood, for old time's sake. The money flowed like water, but we were smart enough to take a cab home so we wouldn't fall on the way and die of exposure. The binge assured monstrous headaches and heaving stomachs for the dawn bus ride to Regina. We'd spent most of our cash.

Despite the hearing's importance, getting to sleep was no problem. I slipped into my familiar coma while Laurie tottered around getting undressed. In fact, I neglected to drink three glasses of water or swallow a couple of 222s, the usual futile remedy against hangover. Seeing my common-law wife trip over chairs in nothing but her pantyhose no longer held the charm it once had. Living with someone does that to you. Oh no, it took dread to turn me on.

Three hours later I woke with a jerk, the way neurotics pop up at dawn. The room was pitch black, and I was sick, as sick as I'd ever been with booze. It wasn't nausea, and I wasn't going to vomit. What I had just been promised would never go away. I'd be fragile for days. The hearing really was going to take place.

Hadn't I realized it? My mouth was foul, I'd be sick all through the trial and I knew I wouldn't sleep properly again. Laurie moved beside me, and I turned my face into her back, feeling tiny scars from acne that still covered her shoulders. I began to kiss her neck. This at least felt like dreaming. She rolled over and I put my tongue in her mouth. She was so warm from sleep, her thighs covered me and I thought I was getting into a bath. She felt gluey between the legs, sluggish. I'd be sick tomorrow, the trial would happen. Laurie moved against me, thick from sleep.

Malcolm was not at the Chateau Prairie, but our old friend Carl was. He shook hands, his toupée remaining straight, and exuded charm. Laurie was hobbling along beside me in a knee-length travelling suit with feet swollen as a grandmother's. Carl offered breakfast.

"Why isn't Malcolm here?" I asked. "Or any of the Elk Brain boys? Nobody told us anything as usual. Where will the hearings take place?"

"Malcolm has nothing to do with this," Carl said, leading us into a dim room with round oak tables where a lot of men in business suits sat alone. The waitresses wore chambermaid costumes – the place obviously doubled as a pub. I noticed baskets of rolls on each table, and thick silverware. The Chateau Prairie was a grand old hotel.

"Malcolm is a prick," I said.

Carl received the news with satisfaction. I probably showed the right fighting spirit for courtroom drama, and I don't think he liked Malcolm.

"By the way, I guess you've heard about Larry," I said. "The situation in the newsroom is hopeless. You'll never get a union there. And Zeke's quit. We don't have any support."

"The hearing today is about your reinstatement," Carl said. "It has nothing to do with certification though, of course, your trying to form a union will figure in the case."

"Are you representing me?"

"No. Ah, there she is now." Carl got up and introduced Laurie and me to a red-headed, short-assed little broad whose glasses were much too large for her. Cindy was our lawyer's name. Carl's old-world manners were a bit nauseating as he pulled out a chair for her and smiled like a courtier. This involved much squeezing and wrinkling of the facial muscles. I was nauseous myself, come to think of it, but still held out hope for what coffee and English muffins might do.

Cindy said she'd brief me later; she was in no hurry, and I agreed. My confidence wavered as she and Carl persisted in making jokes about the provincial civil service, and about what they'd do to the businessmen sharing the dining room with us once they got them to court. The sales managers and oil corporation clerks looked pretty unassailable.

Presumably this self-congratulatory joking was in good fun and I tried to join in. Unfortunately I was too sick. Laurie was silent, resting her swelling feet. I began to find Carl and Cindy rather smug. Even the arrival of bacon and eggs didn't help.

Still and all, what could I do? I had to trust Cindy: she was my lawyer, and I did. When she told Carl and Laurie to wait in the lobby and turned to face me, my heart skipped a beat. Hangover or no hangover, this was it.

"More coffee?" Cindy poured herself a cup from the thermal jug on the table. Her glasses slid down the bridge of her nose.

"Hell, no. What's happening?"

"From what I understand you were told there'd be no repercussions if you didn't cross the picket line. Is that correct?"

"Yep."

"You respected the picket line and you were fired."

"Uh-huh."

"You're positive they said there'd be no repercussions?"

"You're fuckin' right, and I was fired within an hour. I have witnesses, 'cept one of em's dead and the other took off."

"They're simply interfering with your right to support a union. Not to mention joining one. That's all I have to know. Carl's filled me in on the rest of the situation."

"But what will I say in court?"

"It's not a court, it's a hearing."

"But what will I say?"

"Just tell the truth."

"You don't understand. What are our tactics?"

"Tell exactly what happened."

"I'm a bit nervous," I said.

"I don't blame you." Cindy's commiseration was genuine. "I'd hate to be up there."

Instead of unnerving me this sympathy helped. Cindy was honest, and very calm. Still, I expected more of a pep talk.

"Will I be okay?" I wanted to use her first name, but thought that if I did it might rob her of the formal power she had of protecting me. When you have to depend on someone you feel a bit like their child, even if they are a lot smaller than you.

"It's tough. But the other people from the union made out okay."

"How'd they do?" I may not have been panting for reassurance, but my distraction was such that I wasn't listening too well. The last month I'd been so out of touch that I didn't know members of the Elk Brain local had appeared before any labour board.

"They faced questions about the lockout and the IBTP," Cindy said. "Your questions might not be so routine."

"Great."

So our defence was to be the truth. A hope in hell we had.

Carl dropped us off at the Regina Union Centre. He had other business to see to and would not be attending my ordeal. Laurie and I would face the lions alone.

The hearing was to be held in a large hall. A trestle table stretched the width of the room at one end. Here would sit the members of the Labour Board. Two smaller tables faced the main one. These were for counsel. Behind the tables, chairs were scattered about. They looked as if they'd once been lined up in rows. What I presumed to be the witness box was a solitary chair against one wall. We found the opposition waiting.

Bill Pounder, Nick Zudwicki and Tinkus Dixford were seated. The *Tribune's* lawyer, a busy man in steel-rimmed spectacles, was tapping a pencil against his hip and talking to Barbara Birdwell. They were standing. Bill acknowledged me with a slight, yet almost embarrassed smile. I knew he didn't care for me, but the gleam in his eye was civil enough. He looked fat, polished, and harried. Nick was yellow, ashamed and sullen. He stared straight ahead. Tinkus didn't figure, chewing and grinning with idiotic malevolence.

Laurie, Cindy and I went to the other side of the room to take our places. "The Board should be here soon," Cindy leaned over to talk to me. "Stand up when they come in." We quietly ran over the facts again. I felt giddy and very brave. My judges filed in.

One of them had his dog with him, a black Labrador. It was a very old dog and immediately went to sleep under the table. These six men were all in their 50s or early 60s, all wore sports coats, and all looked tired and beaten. They had the usual deeply creased faces, and not from the outdoors. I don't think one of them earned a lot of money.

My lawyer's explanation of the case was restrained, in fact barely audible. During Cindy's presentation I noticed one could see her skull through the halo of red hair. Cindy's synthetic pant suit had a droop in the seat, and I wondered why the folds weren't filled out by swelling buttocks. I know that's contemptible, and that I was on trial with my future at stake, but that's what I was thinking. It's the kind of mind I have. I guess I was under a lot of stress.

The *Tribune's* lawyer was a different matter. Cindy had taken three minutes, he took 15. The man's name was McGregor and he was a talker. His speech, in the debating society manner, was full of 18th-century phrases such as "master-servant relationship". It was the "master" bit that got me. The twerp had me sounding like a runaway bondservant, and what's more *irresponsible*. He did have me feeling guilty, the way a magistrate would make you feel guilty after sentencing. Talk about authority! I was worshipping authority before he was finished. McGregor's attitude made being fired a privilege and I was ungrateful. But if the fucker had me ashamed, he didn't scare me. He didn't scare me because he was a suck.

Suck, as you may know, derives from terms such as sucky baby, to suck a tit, suckhole. It's a label all North American men fear greatly, especially if they wear glasses as McGregor and I did. Now, this McGregor didn't scare me because I knew that if we'd been in the same high school together, he'd have been below me in the social scale. Oh, no doubt his current position of prominence would impress tormenters of former days, but if McGregor was laughable then, he was laughable now. I'd have murdered him in gym class. And though he'd married successfully, given up the chess club, coped with the world far better than I did, though he belonged to law societies and could fill out income tax forms without any help, I was sexier than he was. I was better-looking, more coordinated, and I had him beat.

"Mr. Gogarty, please take the stand."

What? Oh, sure. Up I went.

"Would you explain…" Cindy gave me a nod of encouragement and asked the simple questions we'd rehearsed. What happened on the morning of? What was said? Were you convinced, Mr. Gogarty? This was exactly as she said it would be. I told how I'd gone to work and encountered the picket line. I told how I'd informed Nick I wasn't going to cross, and how all the staff had been assured there'd be no repercussions. I told how I'd been fired. While recounting these tragic events I noticed one of the Labour Board members directing a whimsical sympathy my way. It was the old boy with the dog. He was either looking at me and remembering a fishing trip or totally senile in a bright gay way. He was too kind to be mad. My confidence increased.

McGregor couldn't touch me. I stopped swallowing when in thought about his cross-examination and I stopped answering mechanically. My animation pleased Cindy.

Then I looked at Laurie. Maybe McGregor could get to me after all. I mean, she looked like a matron sitting there in her tweed suit with her swollen feet breaking through her nylons. I remembered the power status had in getting women's pants off, and suddenly I didn't feel sexier than McGregor. His wife may have been much prettier than I thought, and even if she wasn't, he probably had two beautiful daughters or something. If the suckboy wasn't married I bet some secretary or other was after him, someone respectable who'd see me for what I was. Laurie looked like a tenant's wife waiting for news of eviction, sad and powerless, uselessly decent and loyal.

"Mr. Gogarty, are you currently employed?" I woke up quickly. McGregor was on the job. This was what I'd been warned about. His first question was straight out of magistrate's court. I was on trial.

"How could I be? I was told—"

"Never mind what you were told. Answer the question, yes or no."

"That's like asking me do you still beat your wife?" The legal mind of Randy Gogarty was gearing up. I was a match for him all right.

"I assure you it is not," McGregor said. "Please answer the question."

I looked to my coach. Cindy nodded her head. Answer the question.

"No."

"Have you actively sought employment, Mr. Gogarty?"

"How could I? You see…"

"Have you looked for work, Mr. Gogarty?"

"No."

"You have not looked for work since your dismissal?" McGregor raised an eyebrow.

"That's correct." I knew the jargon.

"But you have frequented the Ironwood Hotel since your dismissal?"

"Yes, but I don't see…"

McGregor appealed to the Board, though he was addressing me. "I am only trying to establish some facts, Mr. Gogarty. Do you frequent the Ironwood Hotel?"

"Yes."

"Is it your habit to spend most of your time in taverns instead of seeking employment?"

"Wait a minute. I'm not a drunk."

"Do you remember meeting Mr. Pounder in the Ironwood shortly after the strike."

"Yes, I saw him one night. What was *he* doing there?" I couldn't believe how I was fighting back. Not being a drunk, of course, I was trembling all over the place. But it was a combination of nerves and hangover, not just hangover.

"I suggest you stop looking at your counsel each time you answer a question, Mr. Gogarty."

I hadn't noticed I was doing this, though I'd glanced at Cindy a couple of times to get the go-ahead.

"Did you meet Mr. Pounder at the Ironwood?" McGregor continued.

"Yes."

"Did a conversation take place?"

"I talked to him, yes." I stared at Cindy puzzled.

"Mr. Gogarty, I do not think you or my honourable friend can anticipate my questioning, and," McGregor addressed the Board. "I would like to warn Mr. Gogarty about referring to his counsel."

The chairman of the august body spoke. "Answer the questions yourself, Mr. Gogarty." The old boy with the dog wasn't amused anymore. He kicked Rover under the table. The Lab woke up and looked at me with annoyance. Things were getting tougher than I'd bargained for.

"Now, Mr. Gogarty, do you remember telling Mr. Pounder that you understood his position in 'letting you go', and that you agreed with him?"

"That's not true. I just tried to talk to him, to be human you know, I never said..."

"I take it you were city hall reporter on the *Tribune*?"

"That's correct."

"And this involved covering the city council meetings?"

"Yeah."

"Was it your habit to do this drunk?"

"Wait a minute..."

"I suggest the reason for your dismissal from the *Tribune* was not your ideals, Mr. Gogarty, however Marxist or Maoist they may be."

"No!" I looked to Cindy. She frowned at my excitement.

"Look at me, Mr. Gogarty, I'm asking the questions. I suggest that your last appearance at city council was a drunken one, and that a member of city council, and a radio reporter from CKBM in Elk Brain, can verify your state of intoxication. But first I would like to call Mr. Pounder to the stand to give his version of your encounter at the Ironwood."

Why wasn't my lawyer objecting to these accusations? Cindy looked tense, hugging herself with one arm across her chest as if she was going to tuck up her legs any minute and roll into a neurotic ball.

I stepped down. Big Bill went up, planted his large bottom on the little chair, and lied through his teeth. As he passed our table Bill gave me a look. He was seeking my confirmation in this plot to get me hung. I'm so desperate to be liked I smiled back and gave my consent. Bill was moist and grateful, awkward as a schoolgirl. It was obvious he was ashamed, and I'd never seen his fresh fat face so open.

My former boss said that I'd approached him at the Ironwood, which was true, in order to approve of his "letting me go," which was not true. As a flourish Bill added that I'd confessed to being unhappy out west, having come from the east and all. These head office flunkies were using regionalism against me.

"Would you say Mr. Gogarty was maudlin and drunk on this occasion?"

"He'd had a few drinks, yes."

"A few drinks?"

"Quite a few." Bill nodded regretfully. He hated to admit it.

"That's all."

Next, McGregor called a surprise witness: Mr. Dotswold Goan. A surprise witness to get a nothing like me! The size of a corporation had nothing to do with pettiness.

"What do you make of it?" I whispered.

"It's all right." Cindy wasn't surprised by this meanness, in fact she seemed less distressed than a moment ago.

"They're up to something."

"Yes. Shhh." Cindy wanted to see what was happening. Goan had come out of his hiding place in the corridor and was beginning his testimony.

"Are you familiar with Mr. Gogarty?" McGregor asked his star.

"I am," Goan said, grinning skeletally in his eagerness to please.

"What is the nature of your acquaintance?"

"I'm a member of the Elk Brain city council, have been for years, and Mr. Gogarty was recently the city hall reporter for our local newspaper."

"When was the last time you saw Mr. Gogarty in his capacity as a reporter?"

"Well, it was a few weeks before the strike." Goan crossed his legs as he settled into his story. The shiny cloth of his suit folded comfortably over his bones. "Mr. Gogarty wanted to interview me after a very short meeting. I forget what he wanted. I don't think he knew, because he got his questions mixed up and he smelt very strongly of beer. He told me there would be a newspaper strike, though that was nothing to do with me, and he mentioned he'd been drinking. Yes, he mentioned beer. It was all a big joke to him."

"He was drunk then, while working?"

"Yes. Most definitely."

"Mr. Goan, I take it you are the owner of quite a substantial business in Elk Brain."

"That's right. It's quite a big operation."

"Would you tolerate any employee drinking on the job?"

"Certainly not."

I was ready to jump up and accuse this asshole of sniffing embalming fluid to get high, but McGregor got there before me.

"What is the nature of your business, Mr. Goan."

"I'm a funeral director."

"Have you met Mr. Gogarty in this capacity?"

"I certainly have. A reporter on the *Tribune* recently passed on. Mr. Gogarty and friends came to pay their respects."

"Was this unusual?"

"Not at all, but Mr. Gogarty's behaviour was."

"How so, Mr. Goan."

"He made jokes about embalming. I caught him tampering with the deceased."

"With the body! You're under oath, Mr. Goan."

"It's true. I caught him at the coffin, poking his friend, laughing."

"His friend was the corpse?"

"Yes. It was unseemly and disgusting. He also made jokes about my establishment looking like the Ironwood hotel. I'm a teetotaler."

"It seems Mr. Gogarty is not."

"He was probably drunk." Goan waved a limp and fleshless hand.

"Have you ever encountered such macabre behaviour, Mr. Goan, in all your years as a funeral director?"

"Well, I can truthfully say I haven't."

"Thank you. That's all."

"They're trying to prove I'm nuts," I hissed to Cindy.

"Shhhhh." These distortions didn't seem to worry her.

"They keep saying strike. It was a *lockout*."

"I know. Shhhhh."

The assault continued. McGregor called Barbara Birdwell, wife and mother, to the stand.

Barbara had cut her hair since I'd seen her last, and her hips looked wider, the result of a thick tweed skirt. She and Laurie had a similar sense of style for these occasions. Whether the skirt and its spreading effect was to denote fertility or dowdiness I'm not sure. I also realized that Birdwell had been blessed with a pin head. Getting the hair chopped off emphasized her soft skinny neck, and the way her head perched on the squat sensual body. The lady blushed under questioning; McGregor could have been inquiring about a tipped uterus. Finally she admitted I'd used "bad words" the morning we'd faced the picket line.

"What did he say? You can tell the Board." McGregor was ruthless. If sensibilities had to be offended to get at the truth, then sensibilities had to be offended.

"Randy, uh, Mr. Gogarty, said, said the newsroom staff were, they were..."

"It's all right, Mrs. Birdwell."

Barbara could have been giving birth the way she grunted and groaned.

"He said, uh, he said they were..."

"Yes?" Push down harder.

"He said they were fuckers."

There, it was out, but no one went "Oooo." Barbie could wiggle her toes inside her pumps and go on. "Randy said I'd better stick with the union."

"To ally yourself with the IBTP."

"The union, yes."

"Did you feel he was threatening you, Mrs. Birdwell?"

"In a way, why, yes. And Bill, Mr. Pounder told me that one morning the air had been let out of his tires. I mean what kind of...?"

Mrs. Birdwell's fear and indignation were cut short. Tinkus Dixford, comptroller extraordinaire, was called on to appear.

"This guy's is certifiably insane," I whispered to Cindy. "He can't possibly help them."

"Okay." She was listening attentively, but not to me.

"Tsk." I said. When you're supposed to be important, the figure everyone's discussing, you don't like to be ignored.

Tinkus was not the intellectual fullback of what the *Tribune* probably called its game plan, and McGregor gave him short shrift. It simply established that Larry and I used to drink on the job. Tinkus had seen the empties in our desks. Instead of asking Cindy "What was he doing in my desk?" I had this fantasy of Dixford and Goan waltzing, nude: a comptroller and an undertaker, waltzing, a dance of death to put Goya's cartoons to shame. Meanwhile, Tinkus hummed and hawed, fumbled in his clothing as if about to produce a chocolate bar, and McGregor hustled him off the stand. Tinkus grinned, his compact cheeks glistening beside that lovely nose.

I gave Laurie a nudge and looked at her with tightened lips, this to express our solidarity. Laurie, my matron with her narrow shoulders and thick skirt; Laurie, my whore.

We'd been living too close. I was bored, irritated, and terrifyingly dependent. We were married. I had to get a job.

My eyes shut with helplessness, the deadening helplessness of real unemployment. This charade with the *Tribune* had to work out. I felt a bright thread of rage in the centre of my body.

"Something'll pop up," I said to Laurie. "Something'll pop up."

She stared at me with such stony disbelief that my obligation only increased.

"Something'll pop up." My resentment was close to hatred. "Something'll pop up."

I was hysterical; I was leaden. I really did have to find work; I would not be wanted. Docile, sullen, I did not want to talk to anybody.

"Randy," Cindy interrupted the domestic interlude. "Randy. You're on again."

The first exchange concerned definitions. McGregor kept me busy.

"Were you a member of the union, Mr. Gogarty, at the time the picket line was formed?"

"No, not then."

"Then it was not your strike."

He kept lifting that eyebrow. I wanted to rip it off with my teeth.

"Lockout," I said.

"Strike, Mr. Gogarty." McGregor smiled. "Strike."

Oh, we were amiable all right, except the guy didn't see me. He was all role, and this ludicrous play-acting was dangerous.

"Lockout!" I faced up bravely, acting back, fighting him on his own terms.

McGregor appealed to the Board, infinitely reasonable. "Really, this is not the issue," he said, and went on to defend his use of the word strike for 15 minutes. My jury sat dour and impassive. They must have agreed with McGregor for none of them spoke or made a judgment. My adversary faced me again.

"Why don't you look for work, Mr. Gogarty?" It was a sing-song now, patient but becoming a little short. He turned away and tapped a pen on his desk as I began to answer.

"I wanted to work in my chosen field..."

"What's that?" He was paying attention now.

"...and was advised to await the outcome of this hearing before trying to find another job. If I..."

"Mr. Gogarty!"

"...if I had another job I might not get this one back."

"I repeat, Mr. Gogarty. What is your chosen field?"

"Journalism."

"Do you have training in this field? Did you attend a journalism school?"

"No but..."

"Do you belong to a professional organization?"

"How can I? I work for the *Tribune*, remember?" A masochistic humanism made me smile as I quipped. McGregor dismissed this overture. Friendly gestures had to have more purpose.

"Come on," I said.

"Then you have no experience? No professional credentials?"

We had to do it his way. "I *have* experience. I worked eight months for *Polymer Conglomerate Publications* in Toronto. I..."

"You have no degree, no training, yet the *Tribune* hired you, trained you, and then you decided, for your own reasons, not to do your work."

"We were told we could honour the picket line."

"And not perform your duties?"

"How could I when..."

"May I ask you a question, Mr. Gogarty?"

157

"Go ahead."

"Do you feel you owe an employer anything at all when you work for him."

"Yes, yes I do."

"And what is that, Mr. Gogarty?"

"Why…"

"To work! To work. Mr. Gogarty? To work."

"Yes." I gave up. This bully could tie me in knots and nobody'd say anything. Though he should have been jumping up and down with excitement now he had me, McGregor, ever the professional, just trembled slightly. He paused to pour himself a glass of water.

"Now Mr. Gogarty…" he turned away and lifted the pitcher from his desk.

"Please, sir, may I have some too?"

"Why, certainly." McGregor's broad smile hid his surprise. Tilting his head indulgently, at the Board, at his clients, at his witness, he offered the pitcher. The pantomime didn't work. my point had been made.

"I think we should recess at this point," said the chairman, glancing the length of his fellows, searching for any disagreement. He found none. "We shall reconvene in 15 minutes."

"You were very good," Cindy said as I sat down. "It shouldn't be long now, unless McGregor has more of his tricks."

"Is he a good lawyer?" I asked.

"Put it this way, he doesn't win much."

"Is that his fault, or because of the Labour Board?"

"He does his job."

"Will he win this one?"

"I really don't know," Cindy said.

"Oh." I was downcast, a carry-over of my bit of brilliance on the stand. "Whew," I said, heroically perking up. "It's rough."

I twisted around to stare at Laurie, expecting a response. She was impassive, pinched about the mouth. I don't know if it was because she saw through me, or if it was her usual indifferent hopelessness.

"You were very good," Cindy said.

That's exactly what I wanted to hear.

"I'm going to the can," I said.

"All right. I'll walk you down. I want to see who's in the hall."

There were Board members in the hall, three of them, enjoying their cigarettes, and evidently enjoying the position they were in. These men were not complacent, but the way they chuckled and relaxed reminded me of bureaucrats sharing a joke. The club wasn't one you could join, especially if you were waiting in line. Their laughter wasn't harsh, but still had an echo of the way I'd heard lawyers hooting together outside criminal courts. I felt they were enjoying their jobs too much.

Cindy acknowledged each with a formal, but stridently charming nod. The Board members were large old men, and seemed pleased by her small size and respectful familiarity. We passed them by and stopped at the drinking fountain, murmuring and politely baring our teeth.

One of the group detached himself from his cronies and headed for the men's room. It was the old boy with the dog, and the animal followed, animated and wagging its tail now it was out of the courtroom. The Lab was grinning, and looked like most dogs look when they're happy, rather seedy.

Cindy nodded toward the men's room door, her eyes dewy, watery from all that smiling.

"Should I have a word with him?" I asked.

"It can't hurt. He owns a bookstore. You are interested in books."

I found the old boy taking a leak. His dog had settled into a damp spot in the corner, forlorn again. Obviously, master's leaks were an involved process.

"Whew," I said as I placed myself at a nearby urinal. "It's rough up there."

"Yes, yes it is." The bookseller was tired, grey with fatigue, and it was not the kind of fatigue that came from clawing your way to the top. I liked him immediately.

"Nice dog," I said. What a charmer.

"She's getting on."

"Oh really! How old is she?" I can manoeuvre anybody.

"Thirteen."

"Is that so!"

We lapsed into silence. Neither of us could piss.

"I hear you own a bookstore," I said.

"Yes, I do."

"I like books."

"So do I," and he smiled wanly. "They're important." The man was convinced.

"They are." How could I prove my sincerity?

My potential benefactor was zipping up. The effort of his kidneys had been successful. Regardless of his decision I hoped he saw that I liked books. I'm a sycophant, but an ineffective one. A destructive desire to be genuine, to be liked, always triumphs.

"Books are very important to me," I said as he went out the door. Rover glanced up. Finally I pissed.

The hearing reconvened and McGregor called me back to the stand. He pushed me around for another hour, questioning my abilities as a reporter. He proved I was unsavoury, alcoholic, and artsy. He did not prove I was incompetent. McGregor then took the tack that my very competence was a major offence.

"Are you healthy, Mr. Gogarty?"

"Yes."

"What other kind of work have you done?"

"I worked summers for CNR."

"Doing what?"

"As a labourer."

"Could you do this kind of work again, if you had to?"

"Yes."

"Did you look for this kind of work?"

"No. Why should I? I don't want to be a labourer for the rest of my life. I'm a journalist."

"So it seems. You were hired as a journalist, Mr. Gogarty. Not as a labourer, not as a champion of organized labour, but as a journalist. Once the strike was called did you carry out your duties as city hall reporter?"

"No, I…"

"What other choice did the *Tribune* have, Mr. Gogarty? You were not doing the job you were paid to do, and which you have stressed you were capable of doing."

The trump was Nick, poor, halting, bitter Nick. I noticed lumps in the elbows of his sports coat as he got up to testify. An editor always kept his shirt sleeves rolled up, even under a jacket. Nick used his busy, efficient walk to get to the stand, but he looked as if he'd have been much happier fixing the teletype machine.

McGregor opened with a discussion about Larry, and Larry's ethics.

"He came in nights so he wouldn't have to cross the picket line," Nick said.

"And did he do the job he was paid to do?"

"He wrote his copy." The man of letters twitched.

"Was he fired?" Up went McGregor's eyebrow.

"No. No, Larry wasn't fired." Nick blinked. It was obvious he didn't like the whole business. McGregor didn't keep him long.

"Did you tell Mr. Gogarty he'd be paid if he didn't come to work?"

"I didn't tell him that." Nick wanted to keep his job, and he didn't believe in unions.

It was time for summations.

Cindy kept to the facts. If her recapitulation was sketchy, that was evidence of a desire for clarity. One began to root for her.

My right to aid a union, and this was the law, had been violated. I had been assured there would be no repercussions; I had been fired immediately. Cindy's learned friend had proved there was no reason for me to be fired; I was more than satisfactory as a reporter. "Mr. Gogarty has suffered for months. He should be completely reinstated."

"That'll mean back pay," I said, elbowing Laurie, trying to cheer her up. Cindy should have gone on longer.

My tweedy baby shifted, though I doubted I'd bruised her ribs.

McGregor went on all right; that was to be expected. But his argument was much simpler than Cindy's. He ignored the extraordinary aspects of my character and behaviour, aspects that he'd been at pains to bring out, and hammered and hammered on the fact that I hadn't done my job. "Mr. Gogarty was fired, not because he supported a union, but because he failed to honour the contract he had with the *Tribune*: he refused to work."

Funnily enough McGregor had me feeling guilty. Perhaps it was intimidation, but regardless of what the *Tribune* was, or what they'd done, I felt I owed them something. They had hired me, you see, given me a chance when no one else had. Ottawa wouldn't even look my way, and the slicker media empires had no room for indolent misfits. I had no trade, no skill. The *Tribune* had made me feel

I was worth something, even it if was only $140 a week. I hadn't stabbed them in the back, as McGregor implied, but I wished I'd been able to work all those months. Going back would not be the same.

Then it was over. The Board filed out. Bill smiled sweetly, all was forgiven, and left the hall. Nick rushed after him. He had to get back and write an editorial; I think he was in the middle of a series on *Team Canada*. Goan must have crawled back into the woodwork, because I didn't see him around. Birdwell and Tinkus were in the process of turning their backs and drifting away, Birdwell flashing her fat calves and chattering. They were safe, I was not going to interrupt them, and Tinkus knew this. He grinned with a vast complacency. The conversation was the longest they'd enjoyed for years, and Tinkus rolled his eyes shyly, vacantly, as untouchable as a eunuch. The lawyers were left clearing their desks. I realized what a hangover the excitement had held in check.

"You did real good," Cindy said as she finished packing her brief-case and approached Laurie and I. This echo of Birdwell caused me to look around. The women's editor was long gone.

"Oh sure." Gosh, gee, shucks. Tell me more.

"No. I was quite surprised."

I honoured Laurie with another elbow. She ignored me.

"When will we know the result?" I asked.

"I really can't say."

"Oh, well." Hangover or not, I wanted more compliments. "How'd we do?"

"I really can't say."

"Oh." Pause. "But you think I did well?"

"Yes."

"Do we have a chance?" My voice was nasal with impatience.

"I think so." Cindy was being fair. It wasn't enough.

"How much of a chance?"

"We should go." Laurie began to get up. I dismissed my matron with a glance. What was she so weary for? I was the one who'd been on the stand for three hours.

"I can give you a ride to the hotel," Cindy said.

"That's good. We need some lunch." I looked to my chief supporter for confirmation. Laurie was busy being polite to Cindy with that utterly false smile so frequently used by the lower classes. It was one of those total, back-against-the-wall smiles people use who can't do anything else. My relative, for that's what Laurie felt like at the moment, was embarrassing me. Further cause for annoyance. Her gratitude, this transparent striving for grace, was repellent. When we got to the hotel I started to drink.

The Chateau Prairie boasted a lounge bar and Cap'n Bill's Tavern, as well as the pub where we'd had breakfast. I headed for Cap'n Bill's and ordered two Bo. Trembling I downed them. My hangover eased. I ordered two more and downed them. The tension eased. Laurie sipped a rum Collins and looked away.

"Well then, fuck off," I said to her.

"Come on, Randy." She was being sane.

"I'm sorry. Why don't you order a sandwich."

They didn't have sandwiches, and I had two more Bo. Laurie hardly touched her Collins. We were married; we had nothing to say. I was so dizzy with my own grief I didn't care about her, but I was glad she was there. As I demanded more beer, I noticed a run in her nylons. She was pathetic. For such a young girl her legs were already soft. They had hardly any muscle tone, and they would soon be fat. Her feet were big and sore, and with her knees crossed her thighs had spread and flattened. I wanted to fuck her; I didn't care for her. "More beer." Eventually she got me out of Cap'n Bill's.

Part of our journey to the bus depot stayed with me, the empty streets of Regina, the buildings looking dirty in the cold. The furniture stores were closed. It was Sunday here forever. Wind made my forehead feel like it was bleeding.

I woke on the Greyhound, staring out at thunderheads. They were black, bruise purple in the setting sun. The bus was green inside; there were very few people, and we were bouncing along. Laurie sat tall beside me. Fatigue had collected in the corners of her mouth, a little film. She seemed elderly and grim. I nudged her. She tossed her hair and changed.

CHAPTER THIRTEEN

We won, but by the time the decision was announced it hardly mattered. Cindy called, after the usual delay. The phone rang at four in the afternoon. I wasn't dressed, and hadn't been outdoors in two weeks. Laurie was down at the unemployment, hassling.

The *Tribune* knew all about the Board's ruling. I was to report in on Monday. We'd gotten everything we'd asked for. Accounting would arrange for my back pay.

"Thanks so much, Cindy," I said. "You've helped us and I'm grateful, but it feels like it's come too late."

I changed my underwear and went down to the union centre to tell the boys. Four o'clock in the afternoon and it was dark out.

Walking into the paper on Monday morning was no hell, believe me. It was a long 20 yards back to the newsroom, and I resented the way the Want Ad clerks made a point of noticing me. My passage wasn't accompanied by a hush, but there was a pause and a shocked biting of lower lips. Back to work, girls. I loped along, brash.

Old Marge, the receptionist, made sure she was busy when I came in. Then Bill appeared round a corner, just as he had my first day in Elk Brain. He nodded, but Bill wasn't joking. This was serious business. His frown didn't work and I smiled, pleased with the recognition.

No other greetings were given. The manager's son who had taken over city hall sat in my place, and I was relegated to a desk in the corner. This was Zeke's old domain, and the light didn't work. The time wasn't right to ask about getting it fixed.

Things had really changed. The new city hall reporter may have been a fat slob, but I sensed he was a better journalist than I had been. Zeke's replacement was a pigtailed girl, another fat youngster, who appeared mute. Nick did Larry's job in addition to his own; he'd always liked it. They'd hired a city editor, a sharp-nosed native of Elk Brain featuring rhinestone glasses and an obvious ability to carry a grudge. She hated me. Her name was Doris.

For the next week Doris gave me all the "Hints From Head-quarters" stories. These are a feature of our newspaper chain and they consist of idea sheets mailed out from front office to help city editors with their jobs. Examples: See how the quilting bee is pro-gressing. Okay, westerners, any new cabbage soup recipes? What's left behind in *your* town after the tourists leave? Check the motels. I did stories like this and more, including investigative work on the Salvation Army clothing store.

No one talked to me, of course, and Doris had me cutting copy paper in the basement two days in a row. But circumstances began to improve. The city hall reporter looked my way when he guffawed. The fat chick bit her lips and worked, but glances in my direction showed she was competing. I was a factor. The light on my desk got fixed and Birdwell included me in an order for coffee.

I didn't want to spend the rest of my life anticipating such favours, and I didn't want to work for the *Tribune*. Elk Brain was fin-ished for me. One morning, on my way to work, I realized I hadn't been living in the place for months.

The streets were dark and my friends were gone. Larry was dead; Zeke had left. We'd made no imprint on these cold buildings, they had nothing to do with us anymore. We'd never lived here. The fall, the endless yellow light, was gone. Laurie and I had changed so much. I stepped into a restaurant to get some toast and coffee. The wind was making me sick.

A delay in receiving my back pay was inevitable; the *Tribune* being sure harassment was good for the soul. And I didn't give notice right away. Doris left memos in my typewriter about getting to work at eight sharp, and the strike was settled.

It wasn't a good settlement. I'm not sure the printers and typographers got half of what they wanted, but on the day they came back Malcolm and Wally Ellroy, mouse about town and book-keeper to the EBFL, showed up at my desk. They were elated.

"Pounder's calling me 'sir' all right," Malcolm said. "There's no bullshit now."

Wally allowed his forehead to gleam with pleasure. The office staff turned toward us with the solidarity of disapproval.

"Uh, yeah." I said. Where was their tact? When the mood is on me, and I fear offending, timidity is the closest I get to charm.

"We're having a victory celebration down at the hall tonight," Malcolm said. "Show up."

"Sure," and I smiled weakly at Wally. He was benevolent. Then I caught Doris' insane rhinestone stare. "Sure," I said loudly. The office staff turned back to their jobs and the heralds of organized labour left the premises. That same afternoon a cheque was placed in the bank with my name on it. Back pay, blood money.

Laurie didn't want to attend the celebration. Her experience of the union centre on the night we met, and perhaps a memory of the mural, had left her adamant.

"Okay, honey," I said, feeling as uxorious as only a man with a night off can feel. I hadn't told the missus about quitting yet. It was the secret I used to get through the day, and I hadn't told her about the cheque. One evening at 4 o'clock I'd simply show up with the money. "Let's go, Momma," I'd say, flush.

Party time, party time. The spread was just what Malcolm threatened the night I'd first encountered him, the EBFL and the union centre's regular cuisine. Laid out were roast beef, sweet and sour ribs, steaks, cake, and more. There had been a free bar for 10 minutes, two women trampled, and now drinks sold five to the ticket. Nate and son had done the cooking, and Nate supervised the buffet, large fingers poking at salads, dipping into stews, satisfied as a giant in his great stained apron. The mural was extinguished by the brightness of the supper lights, and we waited for the band.

Everyone came up to congratulate me, and I felt like a symbol. I congratulated myself on how well I was handling this, and I congratulated the union members on our victory. Malcolm, Wally, and I sat at a prominent table and Malcolm, already entertaining us with coma, would lift his head each time my back was slapped. He was taking credit. Wally smiled, pursing his lips and modestly fiddling with his drink.

The musicians showed up. The entertainment committee had gone all out this time. A four-piece orchestra was the order of the day: not your average polka ensemble. The dentured Dvoráks started out with a waltz, the lights went down, and the Bay of Naples glowed on the far wall with joyous radioactivity. These guys could play anything, or so I was informed – waltzes, polkas, rock, and fox trots. Their second number was "Happy Birthday" to someone in the carpenter's union, then I got up to dance.

I'd been drinking boilermakers, and I figured I'd mix with the women even if no one else would. Heroes are tolerated. Bachelor Ellroy followed me up, the men being engaged in serious drinking, but I knew the wives approved. My partner wore a black skirt and silver slippers. This was a formal occasion, in spite of the fact her husband was up north.

All night people came up to ask me how it was going – tired men, men I hadn't met before, men who worked with dangerous chemicals, men overburdened with house payments, men who held two jobs. Wally fetched drinks, swaying as he walked, proper and graceful as a girl. He was accepted. I danced on, a slight embarrassment. But I smiled and joked and cut a figure; I wanted everyone to like me, and they liked me this night. The floor was crowded now, and I sat down to receive more thanks. There were morons who spoke to me, and one or two men, foremen at the mine, I respected so much they made me sad. More drinks. I'll try bourbon.

"Say, where's Carl?" I asked Malcolm when I could get his attention. "Carl the Kraut, ha ha."

"Hot-shotin' it out in B.C. They're going out in Kamloops."

"Well, you'd think he coulda made it for this."

Malcolm gazed at me bleary-eyed. "I guess we did all right by you."

"Yeah, ha ha." The whole thing was a little confusing, especially now, the strike, the victory, my whole life.

"You know what all these men went through?"

"Yeah." Damn him, I wanted to be so gushy and forgiving and friendly, and he was stopping me. I'd gone through shit too. I was the only one who'd supported them, no matter how muddled my motives. I hadn't had any fucking strike pay.

"I guess you owe them a lot," Malcolm said.

From the way they were acting you'd think they owed me a lot.

"Yeah," I said. "Do you want a drink, Malcolm?"

"You got your money all right?"

"Uh-huh."

"Maybe you should buy us a drink."

"I just offered," I said.

"I mean us."

Malcolm was as drunk as a temperance fanatic and he was gazing stupidly around the room.

Now, I'm not a math genius but there were at least 500 people packed into the hall. "Yeah, maybe I should."

"You owe these people a lot."

"Sure." I hesitated, not knowing what else to say. It seemed I was viewing Malcolm through a Vaseline-covered lens. His face was the colour of bourbon.

"Sure," I said. "A drink. Wait a sec. I gotta go to the washroom."

Except for one old legionnaire I was alone in the can. He ignored me and studied himself in the mirror. I waited as he adjusted his blazer, turned round to check the back, and finally left. The room was orange and bright. The porcelain gleamed. I didn't want to go back, back to the smoke and gloom and drinking. It was clear where I was, the light was clear, water was bright when it ran.

Cold entered through the bathroom window that only opened a few inches, and onto an alley. I managed to pull myself up, broke a crust of snow and squeezed through. The powder felt sharp as salt in my eyes and I rolled over. Above the enclosing walls I saw the moon; the air was mineral still. Without bothering to dust myself off I got up and began to run. I ran out of the alley, ran like I always do, but this time I ran home.

My tie flopped and I pumped my knees so high I could have been running on the spot. Down the middle of an icy street in shirt-sleeves, my face concentrated, pompous as a fat child, I must have looked ridiculous. Though I was working hard the temperature made my sweat feel delicate, cool in the hollow of my back. A pale bitterness in the sky hinted of spring.

Laurie looked up from doing her toenails when I burst in.

"Come on, let's go," I panted.

"What?" She kept her hand poised over her foot where she sat on the bed. A small scalpel gleamed. She wasn't having a pedicure; she was paring corns.

"I've run away. I didn't want to tell you, but I got the cheque. It was supposed to be a surprise, and the fuckers down at the union centre wanted me to buy drinks for the house. Fuck that. Let's go."

"Your back pay?"

It must have been so warm in the room, I was red-faced and sweating.

"Laurie." I began to take off my shirt. My skin had flushed pink. She listened and I was grateful.

"This is real. We can go away, I'm not kidding. I've got about $2,000. We can really go away, to Mexico for a while, we can leave. We don't have to stay here. Let's go now, I mean let's go tomorrow morning. I'll get the money. I'll get the money first then quit. You can wait for me at the bus depot. Do you want to come?"

Laurie didn't ask any questions. That great quality can be so irritating. Her face was devoid of makeup. We weren't talking about our relationship, and I didn't cry, though I felt like it. She wasn't there as usual. "Yes," she said. I was happy.

Then we packed and talked: about what we'd do, where we'd go. We were making our getaway. All night we talked in the yellow apartment, brewed tea, read, and finally let the dark come in, making love on top of the bed. The streetlight shone on us. I wasn't sick this time. She was wet, so wet. It felt like another gift.

Our worldly goods fitted into two suitcases, big ones, which Laurie lugged to the bus depot while I went to the bank. With her narrow shoulders and wide floppy hat she looked like someone in a Toulouse Lautrec painting. My errand didn't take me long, and I caught up to her in the waiting room. In spite of the slush and snow, dirty sunlight on the floor assured me winter was over.

There was no problem with the money. I walked over to the *Tribune*, gasped as I so often did on the threshold of that joint, and went back to Nick's desk. He was working on sports.

"I'm quitting."

It was a *fait accompli*. "All right, Randy."

"I'll let you know where to send my pay," checking the door, hoping Malcolm wouldn't appear.

Nick's shirt was dirty; not dirty but an unhealthy grey. Mid-morning and I'd never have anything to do with this place again.

Laurie and I hung around the bus station feeling like fugitives. It was enjoyable, but scary too. I didn't want a confrontation about treachery. There was none.

Leaving the city didn't hurt at all. I knew I'd remember some things about it: driving out onto the prairie one twilight, dreaming of girls and the landscape on a few of the mornings. All the dead time during the strike would go away quickly. I don't really know why I hadn't crossed the picket line, except that Malcolm and his friends, no matter what kind of people they were, didn't seem as dangerous as the management of that paper. A newspaper chain like that, a company like that, is a cold religion. If you work for them, you're always careful, always, and always afraid. I realized now I hadn't liked the way that old typesetter had worked himself to death in a basement. Too much overtime, even if he hadn't complained. Of course, I wasn't thinking of a dead stranger when I saw those guys coming toward me in snowmobile suits, carrying signs. I saw the way Birdwell ignored them, and I didn't like it. We left the city behind.

Our hotel room in Regina was horrible, depressing, and we stayed a day. Mexico quickly paled after I tried to drink like Malcolm Lowry for two days, but I enjoyed being taken care of. Laurie got a tan with her usual indifferent grace, and she stayed with me.

I'm in Saskatoon now, a city with trees. My time out here has been so strange, only staying in Elk Brain nine months, but it feels like I never had much of a life before I came west, and I can hardly remember it. Things were so small back then, my family, my past. They don't seem that way now. I don't know what I'll do, if I'll stay with Laurie, if she'll stay with me, but I've got plans. I do remember the fall when I arrived in Elk Brain, that season, and my friends then. I know I'll probably stay silly and desperate, floating in and out of people's lives, not knowing what I'm doing, but I'll tell you this. I'm looking for a way out now, and that's something.

QUESTIONS FOR DISCUSSION

1. Improbably probable place names inhabit M.T. Kelly's vision of Western Canada (Alder Clump, Saskatchewan, Muskeg, Alaska, not to mention Elk Brain) – compose your own fanciful names for local communities or familiar Canadian locations.

2. Randy has a general BA, Zeke dropped out of journalism school, and Larry is a disk jockey turned sportswriter. What qualifications should a person have to represent themselves as a "journalist?"

3. Randy, Larry, Kitty and Laurie have a fairly *laissez-faire* attitude toward sex. Discuss the ways in which sexual behaviours have changed over half a century.

4. How would you characterize the evolution of the relationship between Randy and Laurie?

5. Compare the similarities and the differences between the handling of the Elk Brain Typesetters Union strike and contemporary workers' strikes.

6. After the long wait for the union settlement, Randy reflects on his motivation for refusing to cross the picket line. He describes the management of the *Tribune* as "dangerous" and the newspaper chain itself as "a cold religion." Are there media companies today that you feel have a similar – or opposite – culture?

7. Make a list of the characters in the book who are most appealing/unappealing to you and consider which actors you would choose to play them in a movie version of *I Do Remember the Fall*.

8. Randy is concerned that people find him "intelligent," thinking that might mean he was "funny" or "odd." He was even more concerned when a young woman called him "effeminate." Compare the perceived implications of words used in the book that could be interpreted as sexist or racist.

9. Considering Randy's experiences in Elk Brain, do you think he stayed in Western Canada? With Laurie? As a journalist? Or did his love of poetry and trains lead him in a different direction?

RELATED READING

Who Has Seen the Wind by W.O. Mitchell

As for Me and My House by Sinclair Ross

Owls in the Family by Farley Mowat

A Complicated Kindness by Miriam Toews

Medicine River by Thomas King

Collected Stories by Rudy Wiebe

A Prairie Year by Jo Bannatyne

THE EXILE CLASSICS SERIES ~ 1 TO 29

THAT SUMMER IN PARIS (No. 1) ~ MORLEY CALLAGHAN
Memoir/Essays 5.5x8.5 280 pages ISBN: 978-1-55096-361-8 (pb) $19.95

It was the fabulous summer of 1929 when the literary capital of North America had moved to the Left Bank of Paris. Ernest Hemingway, F. Scott Fitzgerald, James Joyce, Ford Madox Ford, Robert McAlmon and Morley Callaghan... amid these tangled relationships, friendships were forged, and lost... A tragic and sad and unforgettable story told in Callaghan's lucid, compassionate prose. Also included in this new edition are selections from Callaghan's comments on Hemingway, Joyce and Fitzgerald, beginning in that time early in his life, and ending with his reflection on returning to Paris at the end of his life.

NIGHTS IN THE UNDERGROUND (No. 2) ~ MARIE-CLAIRE BLAIS
Novel 6x9 190 pages 978-1-55096-015-0 (pb) $19.95

With this novel, Marie-Claire Blais came to the forefront of feminism in Canada. This is a classic of lesbian literature that weaves a profound matrix of human isolation, with transcendence found in the healing power of love.

DEAF TO THE CITY (No. 3) ~ MARIE-CLAIRE BLAIS
Novel 6x9 218 pages 978-1-55096-013-6 (pb) $19.95

City life, where innocence, death, sexuality, and despair fight for survival. It is a book of passion and anguish, characteristic of our times, written in a prose of controlled self-assurance. A true urban classic.

THE GERMAN PRISONER (No. 4) ~ JAMES HANLEY
Novella 6x9 64 pages 978-1-55096-075-4 (pb) $13.95

In the weariness and exhaustion of WWI trench warfare, men are driven to extremes of behaviour.

THERE ARE NO ELDERS (No. 5) ~ AUSTIN CLARKE
Stories 6x9 159 pages 978-1-55096-092-1 (pb) $17.95

Austin Clarke was one of the most significant writers of our times. These are compelling stories of life as it is lived among the displaced in big cities, marked by a singular richness of language true to the streets.

100 LOVE SONNETS (No. 6) ~ PABLO NERUDA

Poetry 5.5x8.5 250 pages ISBN: 978-1-55096-387-8 (pb) $27.95

As Gabriel García Márquez stated: "Pablo Neruda is the greatest poet of the 20th century – in any language." And this is the finest translation available, anywhere!

THE SELECTED GWENDOLYN MACEWEN (No. 7)
GWENDOLYN MACEWEN

Poetry/Fiction/Drama/Art/Archival 6x9 352 pages
ISBN: 978-1-55096-111-9 (pb) $32.95

"This book represents a signal event in Canadian culture." —*Globe and Mail*
The only edition to chronologically follow the astonishing trajectory of MacEwen's career as a poet, storyteller, translator and dramatist, in a substantial selection from each genre.

THE WOLF (No. 8) ~ MARIE-CLAIRE BLAIS

Novel 6x9 124 pages ISBN: 978-1-55096-105-8 (pb) $19.95

A human wolf moves outside the bounds of love and conventional morality as he stalks willing prey in this spellbinding masterpiece and classic of gay literature.

A SEASON IN THE LIFE OF EMMANUEL (No. 9) ~ MARIE-CLAIRE BLAIS

Novel 6x9 175 pages ISBN: 978-1-55096-118-8 (pb) $19.95

Widely considered by critics and readers alike to be her masterpiece, this is truly a work of genius comparable to Faulkner, Kafka, or Dostoyevsky. Includes 16 ink drawings by Mary Meigs.

IN THIS CITY (No. 10) ~ AUSTIN CLARKE

Stories 6x9 221 pages ISBN: 978-1-55096-106-5 (pb) $21.95

Clarke has caught the sorrowful and sometimes sweet longing for a home in the heart that torments the dislocated in any city. Eight masterful stories showcase the elegance of Clarke's prose and the innate sympathy of his eye.

THE NEW YORKER STORIES (No. 11) ~ MORLEY CALLAGHAN

Stories 6x9 158 pages ISBN: 978-1-55096-110-2 (pb) $19.95

Callaghan's great achievement as a young writer is marked by his breaking out with stories such as these in this collection... "If there is a better storyteller in the world, we don't know where he is." —*New York Times*

TOTAL REFUSAL/REFUS GLOBAL: THE COMPLETE 1948 MANIFESTO (No. 12) ~ THE MONTRÉAL AUTOMATISTS

Manifesto 6x9 142 pages ISBN: 978-1-55096-107-2 (pb) $21.95

The single most important social document in Quebec history, and the most important aesthetic statement a group of Canadian artists has ever made. This is basic reading for anyone interested in Canadian history or the arts in Canada.

TROJAN WOMEN (No. 13) ~ GWENDOLYN MACEWEN

Drama 6x9 142 pages ISBN: 978-1-55096-123-2 (pb) $19.95

A trio of timeless works featuring the great ancient theatre piece by Euripides in a new version by MacEwen, and the translations of two long poems by the contemporary Greek poet Yannis Ritsos.

ANNA'S WORLD (No. 14) ~ MARIE-CLAIRE BLAIS

Novel 5.5x8.5 166 pages ISBN: 978-1-55096-130-0 $19.95

An exploration of contemporary life, and the penetrating energy of youth, as Blais looks at teenagers by creating Anna, an introspective, alienated teenager without hope. Anna has experienced what life today has to offer and rejected its premise. There is really no point in going on. We are all going to die, if we are not already dead, is Anna's philosophy.

THE MANUSCRIPTS OF PAULINE ARCHANGE (No. 15) MARIE-CLAIRE BLAIS

Novel 5.5x8.5 324 pages ISBN: 978-1-55096-131-7 $23.95

For the first time, the three novelettes that constitute the complete text are brought together: the story of Pauline and her world, a world in which people turn to violence or sink into quiet despair, a world as damned as that of Baudelaire or Jean Genet.

A DREAM LIKE MINE (No. 16) ~ M.T. KELLY

Novel 5.5x8.5 174 pages ISBN: 978-1-55096-132-4 $19.95

A Dream Like Mine is a journey into the contemporary issue of radical and violent solutions to stop the destruction of the environment. It is also a journey into the unconscious, and into the nightmare of history, beauty, and terror that are the awesome landscape of the Native American spirit world.

THE LOVED AND THE LOST (No. 17) ~ MORLEY CALLAGHAN
Novel 5.5x8.5 302 pages ISBN: 978-1-55096-151-5 (pb) $21.95

With the story set in Montreal, young Peggy Sanderson has become socially unacceptable because of her association with black musicians in nightclubs. The black men think she must be involved sexually, the black women fear or loathe her, yet her direct, almost spiritual manner is at variance with her reputation.

NOT FOR EVERY EYE (No. 18) ~ GÉRARD BESSETTE
Novel 5.5x8.5 126 pages ISBN: 978-1-55096-149-2 (pb) $17.95

A novel of great tact and sly humour that deals with ennui in Quebec and the intellectual alienation of a disenchanted hero, and one of the absolute classics of modern revolutionary and comic Quebec literature. Chosen by the Grand Jury des Lettres of Montreal as one of the 10 best novels of post-war contemporary Quebec.

STRANGE FUGITIVE (No. 19) ~ MORLEY CALLAGHAN
Novel 5.5x8.5 242 pages ISBN: 978-1-55096-155-3 (pb) $19.95

Callaghan's first novel – originally published in New York in 1928 – announced the coming of the urban novel in Canada, and we can now see it as a prototype for the "gangster" novel in America. The story is set in Toronto in the era of the speakeasy and underworld vendettas.

IT'S NEVER OVER (No. 20) ~ MORLEY CALLAGHAN
Novel 5.5x8.5 190 pages ISBN: 978-1-55096-157-7 (pb) $19.95

1930 was an electrifying time for writing. Callaghan's second novel, completed while he was living in Paris – imbibing and boxing with Joyce and Hemingway (see his memoir, Classics No. 1, *That Summer in Paris*) – has violence at its core; but first and foremost it is a story of love, a love haunted by a hanging. Dostoyevskian in its depiction of the morbid progress of possession moving like a virus, the novel is sustained insight of a very high order.

AFTER EXILE (No. 21) ~ RAYMOND KNISTER
Poetry 5.5x8.5 240 pages ISBN: 978-1-55096-228-4 (pb) $19.95

This book collects for the first time Knister's poetry. The title *After Exile* is plucked from Knister's long poem written after he returned from Chicago and decided to become the unthinkable: a modernist Canadian writer. Knister, writing in the Twenties and Thirties, could barely get his poems published in Canada, but magazines like *This Quarter* (Paris), *Poetry* (Chicago), *Voices* (Boston), and *The Dial* (New York City), eagerly printed what he sent, and always asked for more – and all of it is in this book.

THE COMPLETE STORIES OF MORLEY CALLAGHAN (Nos. 22-25)

Four Volumes ~ Stories 5.5 x 8.5 (pb) $19.95 each volume
v1 ISBN: 978-1-55096-304-5 352 Pages
v2 ISBN: 978-1-55096-305-2 344 Pages
v3 ISBN: 978-1-55096-306-9 360 Pages
v4 ISBN: 978-1-55096-307-6 360 Pages

The complete short fiction of Morley Callaghan is brought together as he comes into full recognition as one of the singular storytellers of our time. "Attractively produced in four volumes, each introduced by Alistair Macleod, André Alexis, Anne Michaels and Margaret Atwood, and each containing 'Editor's Endnotes.' The project is nothing if not ambitious... and provides for the definitive edition."
—*Books in Canada*

And, so that the reader may appreciate this writer's development and the shape of his career – and for those with a scholarly approach to the reading of these collections – each book contains an on-end section providing the year of publication for each story, a Questions section related to each volume's stories, and comprehensive editorial notes. Also included are historical photographs, manuscript pages, and more.

CONTRASTS: IN THE WARD ~ A BOOK OF POETRY AND PAINTINGS (No. 26) ~ LAWREN HARRIS

Poetry/16 Colour Paintings 7x7 168 pages
ISBN: 978-1-55096-308-3 (special edition pb) $24.95

Group of Seven painter Lawren Harris's poetry and paintings take the reader on a unique historical journey that offers a glimpse of our country's past as it was during early urbanization. "This small album of poetry, paintings, and biographical walking tour ought to be on every 'Welcome to Toronto' (and 'Canada') book list. Gregory Betts's smart, illustrative writing, which convinces by style as well as content, and Exile Editions' winning presentation, combine to make *Lawren Harris: In the Ward* a fresh look at the early work of one of Canada's most iconic modernists." —*Open Book Toronto*

WE WASN'T PALS ~ CANADIAN POETRY AND PROSE OF THE FIRST WORLD WAR (No. 27) ~ ED. BRUCE MEYER AND BARRY CALLAGHAN
Poetry/Prose 5.5x8.5 320 pages ISBN: 978-1-55096-315-1 (pb) $18.95

For decades the literature of Canada's experience in World War One lay ignored and was dismissed by readers, critics, and literary historians. Here, at last, is the imaginative testimony of those who served in the trenches and hospitals of the Great War. These pages chronicle the struggle to put into words the horrors, the insights, and the tribulations that ultimately shaped a nation's character. In the voices of Frank Prewett, W. Redvers Dent, nurse Berta Carveth, fighter pilot Hartley Munro Thomas, and other members of a generation that gave their lives and their souls to the war, this is the first anthology since 1918 of poetry, fiction, essays, songs, and illustrations that adds an important new chapter to Canada's literature. Preface and Introduction by Bruce Meyer; Foreword by Barry Callaghan; Afterword by Margaret Atwood.

LUKE BALDWIN'S VOW (No. 28) ~ MORLEY CALLAGHAN
Novel 5.5x8.5 196 pages ISBN: 978-1-55096-604-6 (pb) $19.95

A timeless classic, highly recommended by generations of readers and educators. A story of a boy and his dog and their adventures, which will appeal to the many children – and adults – who are dog lovers. It is also a sensitive story of love and loss, and of making a new life for oneself. Although it was first published 70 years ago, only a few details (such as clothing) really indicate that it is not a contemporary story.

COYOTE CITY / BIG BUCK CITY (No. 29) ~ DANIEL DAVID MOSES
Two Plays 5.5x8.5 220 pages ISBN: 978-1-55096-678-7 (pb) $24.95

A respected First Nations playwright and Governor General's Award finalist, Daniel David Moses is known for using storytelling and theatrical conventions to explore the consequences of the collision between Indigenous and non-Indigenous cultures. *Coyote City* and *Big Buck City* are the first two in his series of four City Plays that track the journey of one particular Native family between a world of Native spiritual traditions and the materialist urban landscape in which we all attempt to survive. *Coyote City*, a tragedy, begins with a phone call from a ghost that sends a young Native woman, Lena, and her family on a search in the city for her missing lover, Johnny. *Big Buck City*, a farce, tells the story of Lena's subsequent Christmas reunion in that city with her family just in time for the birth of her own miraculous child.